SILENT WINTER
SOLSTICE

SILENT WINTER SOLSTICE

A BETH AND EVIE MYSTERY: BOOK 1

BONNIE OLDRE

gatekeeper press
Columbus, Ohio

This book is a work of fiction. The names, characters, and events in this book are the products of the author's imagination or are used fictitiously. Any similarity to real persons living or dead is coincidental and not intended by the author.

Silent Winter Solstice

Published by Gatekeeper Press
2167 Stringtown Rd., Suite 109
Columbus, OH 43123-2989
www.GatekeeperPress.com

The cover design, interior formatting, typesetting, and editorial work for this book are entirely the product of the author. Gatekeeper Press did not participate in and is not responsible for any aspect of these elements.

Library of Congress Control Number: 2023937420

ISBN (paperback): 9781662916533
eISBN: 9781662916540

Contents

Acknowledgments vii

Chapter 1. 1

Chapter 2. 13

Chapter 3. 22

Chapter 4. 30

Chapter 5. 38

Chapter 6. 52

Chapter 7. 58

Chapter 8. 66

Chapter 9. 75

Chapter 10 82

Chapter 11 94

Chapter 12 105

Chapter 13 114

Chapter 14 125

Chapter 15 132

Chapter 16 143

Chapter 17 154

Chapter 18 167

Chapter 19 176

Chapter 20 187

Chapter 21 198

Chapter 22 206

Chapter 23 221

Chapter 24 229

Chapter 25 239

Chapter 26 246

Chapter 27 254

Chapter 28 261

Chapter 29 269

Biography. 283

Acknowledgments

I want to thank The Third Saturday Writers' Group. We first met while taking a novel-writing class at the Loft Literary Center, in 2018. With a few additions and subtractions over the years, we have continued to meet. Their insights and encouragement have been invaluable in adding companionship and fun to the sometimes lonely pursuit of writing.

I especially want to thank my first reader and husband, Randy Oldre. His enthusiastic requests for the next chapters kept me busily writing, so he could keep reading to find out what happened next and who did it.

Chapter 1

December 21, 1968

I'm going to be late, Beth Williams thought, as she hurried along the icy gravel access road running along the base of the railroad berm, through Davison City's Central Park. She glanced at her Timex watch, a gift from her parents when she'd graduated from high school, a dozen years ago. It was almost four in the afternoon. The sun was starting to set, streaking the sky pink and purple, and the shadows had lengthened. It got dark early in northwestern Minnesota on the shortest day of the year.

Where are the kids? she wondered. Christmas break had just started and they should be out playing, laughing, and whooping as they slid down the hill, or making endless circuits around the ice-skating rink. She looked around at the trampled snow and the deserted rink illuminated by lights, high above it on poles, which glistened off the scratched surface.

Then she remembered that this morning Apollo 8 had taken off on the first manned mission to orbit the moon. If

1

all went as planned, they would arrive on Christmas Eve, orbit the moon ten times, and then return to Earth. She glanced up at the rising moon and wondered where they were now. She guessed that the kids not glued to their TV sets watching news coverage of the space flight were getting ready to perform in Christmas pageants.

Beth was on her way to her Saturday evening shift at the public library. The shortcut through the park shaved a few minutes off the trip, and every minute counted. She pictured Miss Tanner sitting at the checkout desk, tapping her polished nails and glancing at the clock. When she came through the front doors, Miss Tanner would purse her lips and her dyed-red, bouffant hairdo would quiver in indignation as she glanced dramatically up at the large round clock on the wall and announced, "Running a little late, today, are we?"

Beth's thin coat flapped open in the sharp wind. *Damn, it's cold*, she thought, as she burrowed her hands into her coat pockets and pulled it close. *Why didn't I go get my winter coat and boots?* They were at her parents' house. She'd moved back home last summer after the big breakup with Ernie. She grimaced in disgust at the thought of him. When her mother told her about a job opening up in the Davison City Public Library, where she'd worked during high school, she'd decided the time was right for a fresh start. She'd researched Library Science programs and found one at North Dakota State College.

Inspired by Beth's plans, her best friend, Evie Hanson, had decided to enroll in college, too, and get a BFA degree. She'd always loved art and had talked about going back to school for years, but it hadn't seemed practical. With Beth's and her parents' encouragement, she'd decided to go for it. She quit her practical, but dull, job in the office of the local sugar beet plant and was now a full-time student. Which was great for Beth, because they could drive together, and Beth's car was currently out of commission.

Beth had stayed in her old bedroom for a few months after moving back home. Her mom wanted her to stay, but she wasn't ready for that level of hovering, care, and concern. It seemed to Beth that her mom was more distraught over her breakup with Ernie than she was. Once she'd accepted the idea that it was over, that he was just stringing her along and was never going to pop the question, she'd ended their relationship. She had been kind of relieved. She realized that the life of a doctor's wife wouldn't have suited her.

To maintain a bit of independence from her parents, she'd rented her own apartment a few blocks away from her parents' house. Unfortunately, she'd left some stuff behind when she moved out, including her winter clothes. She'd intended to pick them up today because the temperature was predicted to dip below zero tonight. But then the phone rang, and she got into a lengthy conversation with Evie about final exams and term papers. Suddenly, she realized it was late and she had to rush off to work.

Beth slipped, and did a sort of jig, flailing her arms around to stay on her feet. The soles of her penny loafers were worn smooth and provided no traction. She managed to stay upright but felt a run in her stocking buzz up her right leg. She looked down at a gaping hole in her nylons exposing a plump, pink knee.

"Damn it! That's all I need," she cried out, her voice echoing in the stillness.

Now she'd have to spend all evening trying to hide the hole in her stocking. It was too late to go home and change. Her miniskirt, which didn't flatter her size-16 body, wouldn't hide her knees. She strategized. *I'll stay behind the circulation desk as much as possible, and cross my legs to try to conceal the tear. I'll take off my coat and hold it in front of me as I enter the library. No point in giving Miss Tanner another reason to belittle me.*

A rustling and whooshing sound distracted her and she looked around to find the source. All she saw was a trampled expanse of snow covering the irregularly shaped park lying between the frozen Rust Lake River to her left, and the railroad berm to her right. The swings on the playground moaned softly and waved in the wind. *That must have been what I heard,* she decided.

She glanced at her watch again. *I have to get organized one of these days, or I'll lose my job.* And then what? Without her job, she'd have to move back home. Her little apartment, on the first floor of a crumbling old duplex, wasn't much, but it was her little piece of independence, and she intended to keep it. More importantly, this Library Assistant job was the first step in her newly selected career.

While growing up, she'd assumed she would be living a much more glamorous life by 30 years old. As a kid, she'd dreamed of being a stewardess flying to exotic locations, a go-go dancer, a model, or even an astronaut. She smiled at the last one, knowing it was the dream least likely to come true. But who knows? It would be a decade or two until astronauts went to Mars, and she would like to be one of the first to volunteer. It would be nice to "slip the surly bonds of Earth." It had gradually dawned on her that stewardesses, go-go dancers, and models all had to be much thinner than she would ever be, and she had a hard time completing the minimum college requirements for science and math. So much for being an astronaut.

Her favorite fantasy was becoming a writer. She would live in a big house filled with antiques, dark wood, and leather furniture. She would sit in front of a fireplace and sip wine when she wasn't flying off to New York to have lunch with her agent or editor, or jet-setting around the world. But, it would be a long time, maybe forever, before she realized that dream.

For the time being, working on a master's degree, keeping her job in the library, and taking care of her new pet cat and her apartment took all of her time and attention. She increased the tempo of her walk, pumping her arms and swinging her purse back and forth.

Miss Tanner hated tardiness, but she hated working evenings even more, and she trusted Beth to staff the library and to lock up at closing time. Beth wondered where she rushed off to every evening. Probably just a trip to the Red Owl or Piggly Wiggly, followed by an evening of watching Gunsmoke

or Bonanza. But, who knows? Miss Tanner wasn't the sort of
person who invited personal questions. While in high school,
Beth had worked at the library for over a year before she learned
Miss Tanner's first name was Olivia. She'd overheard a man
call her that one time. A tall, serious-looking man in a tweed
suit stopped by the library to pick her up. Later, Miss Tanner
said it was her brother. But, according to Beth's dad, she didn't
have a brother.

A flash of movement over her shoulder caught Beth's eye
and interrupted her ruminations. She glimpsed a dark shape
above, on the railroad tracks, but it disappeared before she got
a good look. Had someone been up there, watching her? But
why would they? No, it was probably a railroad employee out
for a smoke or someone waiting for a train. She scrutinized
the hill leading up to where the person had been standing and
noticed a path in the snow leading down the hill. That wasn't
odd—there were numerous sledding paths. But, there was
something unusual about this one. The edges were ragged,
not smooth as you would expect from a sled, toboggan, or
even a piece of cardboard, and there was something at the
bottom of it.

Should she investigate? She glanced at her watch—a couple
of minutes past four. She was already late; a few more minutes
wouldn't matter. She hurried back toward the bundle, sliding
her feet along the ground in an animated shuffle to prevent
another slip. When she got closer, she saw what seemed to be a
bundle of clothes. That was odd. She stepped off the road and
into the snow, which went past her ankles and halfway up her

shins, filling her shoes with snow. Fully intent on her search, she ignored the cold and drew closer.

There seemed to be white things sticking out of the bundle. The lengthening shadows made it hard to make sense of what she was seeing. She reached down and touched it. The bundle rolled another half turn, and then she saw a face gazing up at her. It was a girl. She started back and cried out in horror. The girl lay on her back now, eyes wide open but unseeing. Beth had never seen a dead person, except for her grandfathers at their funerals, but she immediately knew this girl was dead. She stumbled backward toward the road, her hands over her mouth to suppress a scream. She couldn't take her eyes off the girl. She seemed familiar, for some reason.

What should she do? Beth looked around. No one was in sight. She looked up. There was the railroad station. Should she try to run up the hill to it? She probably couldn't make it in her slippery shoes. Trying and failing would only waste time. She turned and broke into a run, heading toward the library, still a couple of blocks away.

She fell a couple of times, but sprang back up and continued running. She sprinted up the two staircases of the Carnegie library, past the four columns and the two globe lights illuminating the entrance, and burst, panting, through the double doors, followed by a gust of cold air.

Miss Tanner sat behind the circulation desk in the center of the main reading room. Her expression transformed from annoyance to amazement as she gazed at Beth, panting and disheveled, in front of her. Forgetting to use her library voice, she blurted out, "Beth, what on earth is the matter?"

"Call the police!"

"Why? What's happened?"

"I found a body."

Miss Tanner looked around anxiously, and motioned for Beth to come closer. A couple of school kids stopped reading and stared in their direction. Beth rounded the corner of the circulation area and went through the gate that separated it from the rest of the room.

"Are you sure?" Where did you see this?" Miss Tanner's voice was low and urgent.

"In the park, just now. I was on my way here. And, and..." Beth panted. "I saw someone roll something down the hill. I went to look. It was a body. Please, we can't waste any more time. You have to call. Now!" Beth heard her voice rising, and felt a bubble of hysteria rising in her chest.

"Calm down. I'll go into the office and call the police. You stay here. Okay?" Miss Tanner headed through the stacks toward the back of the library. Her high-heeled shoes rat-a-tatting as she hurried along the marble-tiled floor.

Beth slumped down into a chair, took deep breaths, and tried to calm down. She noticed the hole in her stocking. She'd temporarily forgotten all about it, and arranged her coat over it. One of the kids who had been sitting in the periodical section approached the desk and leaned toward Beth.

Bobby Daniels was about twelve years old, with freckles that stood out on his pale skin, and rust-colored hair sticking up all over his head as if he had pulled off a stocking hat and had left it that way. His bright blue eyes were wide with curiosity.

"Did you find a body?" he whispered.

"No...That is, I'm not sure."

"You said you found a body," he said loudly.

"Shh." She put her finger up to her lips.

"I heard you say it. You said you found it. I heard you," he whispered, leaning over the circulation desk toward her.

"Yes, well, I thought so." She wasn't sure how to discourage this inquisitive little pest. "We'll see. It's a grown-up matter. Now, go back to your reading," she said, trying to sound as official as possible.

He scurried back to his table, and soon several kids, heads huddled together, leaned on their elbows on the table, whispered loudly, and cast wondering looks in her direction.

Oh, great. It'll be all over town by morning, she thought. Suddenly, aware of the snow melting in her shoes, she kicked them off and thumped the snow out of them and into the metal trash can under the desk.

Miss Tanner returned to the circulation desk, and said in a low voice, "I have the police on the line. They have a lot of questions. You'd better go talk to them." She looked Beth up and down, staring at her over her horn-rimmed glasses attached to a beaded eye-glass chain. "And take some time to freshen up before you return. You are a bit disheveled, my dear. I'll stay a little later tonight."

Beth thought she detected a slight smile and a tone of enthusiasm in Miss Tanner's voice. She went into the librarian's office, closed the door behind her, and picked up the phone. "Hello."

"This is Officer Crample. Is this Elizabeth Williams?"

Beth was momentarily taken aback. No one called her by her full name, except the nuns when she was in grade school. It was always Beth. "Yes, this is she."

"I spoke to Miss Tanner. She said you claimed to have found a body in the park. Is that right?"

"Yes, that's correct," she said. *Why would he say, "claimed"?* she wondered. *Is that how cops talk, or does he think I go around claiming I've found bodies regularly?*

"Where and when, exactly?"

"At the bottom of the railroad hill. In Central Park. Around 4:00 this evening."

"What were you doing there at that time?"

"I was walking through the park on my way to work. Here, at the library. It's a shortcut. I go that way often." Did she sound defensive? She wondered why he was asking all these questions. "You should probably hurry. There was a man at the top of the hill. I saw him. That is, I think I saw him. He's probably gone by now, though."

"I see. Okay, miss, we'll send a car over there to take a look. We might have some additional questions later. Where can we reach you?"

She gave him the library's phone number, told him they closed at eight, and gave him her home address and phone number. He asked for another number where she could be reached, so she gave him her parents' phone number, too. When she hung up, there was a damp spot on the receiver. She grabbed the bottom edge of her sweater cuff with the tips of her fingers and wiped it off. Talking to the police made her nervous. *Probably because it was new to me,* she thought, *or maybe because he sounded so skeptical.*

She checked her reflection in the small mirror on the office wall. Her cheeks were bright pink from the cold. She fished a small comb out of her purse and tried to smooth down the shoulder-length, light-brown hair that floated around her face in all directions due to static electricity, and rearranged her headband to control it as best she could. She wondered about the hole in her stocking and decided to keep her coat on to better hide it and say she was chilly if asked.

It was true that every time the door opened, a gust of wind blew right across the circulation desk. She wished that Miss Tanner would allow her to wear slacks. Not only did it make for a warmer walk, but also it saved money on hosiery. No matter how careful she was, they never lasted more than a week or two, and took a big bite out of her slim salary. But Miss Tanner was in her fifties, she guessed, and had old-fashioned ideas about what was and wasn't appropriate work wear.

There wasn't much she could do about her soggy shoes. She'd just have to suffer. Maybe she could get her dad to come and give her a ride after work, so she wouldn't freeze her feet on the way home. She left the door of the office open so she could hear the phone if the police called back for more information, and headed back to the circulation desk.

Chapter 2

The pounding on the door sent Chestnut, the cat, from where he'd been sleeping next to Beth, flying up in the air and scuttling under the bed. She rolled over and groggily checked the alarm clock. It was 8:10 on a Sunday morning. Who would be rude enough to arrive at that hour, without as much as a phone call?

After a brief pause, the pounding began again. Wide awake now, Beth slipped out of bed, hurriedly tied her fluffy robe around her, and scurried across cold linoleum floors in her bare feet. She opened the door a crack and, seeing a police officer in the doorway, opened it all the way, letting in gusts of cold air.

"Miss Williams?"

"Yes, she nodded while pushing her bed-head hair back with one hand.

"I'm Officer Crample—Bill Crample." He flipped open an ID in front of her face. "Can I come in?"

Beth hopped from foot to foot as her feet froze. She hesitated for a moment, examining the man in her doorway. He was young, thirty-something, but balding. His scalp showed beneath his close-cropped brown hair. There was an air of unreality about the scene—like something you'd see on TV. Fleetingly, she wondered how she could be sure he was showing her a genuine ID. However, she'd seen him patrolling around town, so she knew he was a cop. Until now, she hadn't known his name.

"Sure," she said, stepped aside, waved him in, and hurriedly closed the door.

"I have some follow-up questions from your call last night," he said. His leather jacket creaked as he pulled out a pencil and a small notebook.

"Okay, but you woke me up. I need to take care of a few things. You know, get dressed and stuff."

"Take your time." He grimaced in what, she supposed, was meant to be a smile.

"Take a seat." She gestured toward a blanket-covered couch, battered armchair, and cluttered coffee table. That, along with a TV set sitting on a boards-and-blocks bookshelf surrounded by paperbacks, made up the furnishings of her living room. "I'll be right back."

She returned a few minutes later, after hastily freshening up and jumping into jeans, a sweatshirt, and socks. Officer Crample was sitting on the couch, leaning forward as it sagged under his weight, trying to entice Chestnut out from under the bookshelves, where he crouched and warily surveyed this intruder.

"Coffee?" she asked. "I'm going to start some."

"Okay, I guess so."

"I only have instant, I'm afraid. It's pretty awful, but it'll warm you up, I suppose."

"It is cold out there, that's for sure," he said.

After they settled in, each with a mismatched mug in hand, he said, "I wanted to check with you about where you said you saw that dead girl last night." He took a slurp and set the mug down, carefully, between piles of books, magazines, and newspapers, and opened his notebook.

"At the bottom of the hill in the park," she said.

Crample carefully recorded her response in the notebook with the pencil stub.

"Where, exactly? Do you remember?"

She stopped to visualize it. Chestnut came over and rubbed up against her legs while purring. Suddenly, he jumped up into her lap, nearly causing her to spill her coffee. But she was used to his habits and managed to move it in time.

"I guess he likes you," he said, nodding toward the cat.

"He wants me to feed him," she said, petting the brown and tan striped cat who kneaded her legs with his front claws.

"What's his name?"

"This is Chestnut. Say hi, Chestnut," she said in a high-pitched, talking-to-my-pet voice. Chestnut ignored her.

"What did she look like, this girl?" Crample asked.

Beth paused to consider. "Young, maybe late teens or early 20s, blond, blue-eyes." She visualized the wide-open, staring eyes with a shiver. "Um, let me think. I don't know what she was wearing. A long coat and skirt, I think."

"A long skirt? I thought girls were wearing short skirts now," he said.

"Some girls wear them long. Like a maxiskirt. Or maybe she was coming from a party or something. I got the impression of a lot of clothing. At first, I thought it was a bundle of clothes that someone had tossed down the hill until I went to take a closer look."

Crample carefully noted "maxiskirt" in his notebook, mouthing the words as he wrote them.

"So the location—you mean the railroad hill?"

"Uh-huh." She nodded. "As I recall, it was just past the back of the railroad station. I remember because I thought about running up the hill to use the phone to call the police, but I thought that I might not make it up the hill in my slippery shoes, so I ran to the library and called from there, instead."

"Huh, that's funny because we went over there in a patrol car after you called last night, and I went back again this morning before I stopped here, and I didn't see nothing." He stared at her, narrowing his eyes as if to catch her in a lie.

"What?" She sipped her coffee, thinking for a moment. "I don't know. Maybe the snow covered her up."

"Could you point out the spot where you think you saw the body?"

"Maybe. I was in a hurry because I was running late for work, but I think I have a pretty good idea."

"Should we go over there, now, and take a look?" he asked.

"Right now? Sure, I guess so." She hurriedly gulped coffee and got up. Chestnut jumped down and meowed a protest at being dislodged from his perch. "Just let me feed the cat first, and then we can go."

After a short drive, Crample parked the squad car next to the ice-skating warming house. Several hockey players were already on the ice, even though the warming house wasn't open yet. Their skates scritch-scratched as they raced across the ice, and hockey pucks banged into the sideboards. They paused to watch as Officer Crample and Beth got out of the patrol car and crunched across the snow toward the place where she'd seen the body fall down the hill the night before.

He gave her a sidelong look. "Aren't you cold?"

"Yes." She shivered in the early morning sub-zero cold, turned up her collar, stuck her hands into her pockets, and pulled her lightweight coat around her. Her ears and face started to tingle. "I have to go pick up my winter coat and other things from my parents' house today."

"Did you forget that winter was coming this year?"

"Ha, ha," she forced a laugh. "No, I had things on my mind. Final exams and stuff."

She rushed ahead, gazing up toward the railroad station, scanning the hill for signs of the place the body had rolled down the hill last night or where it might be hidden at the bottom in a heap under a snowdrift. Everything looked different in the early morning light. The sun glistened off the snow, obscuring the outline of the path down the hill that she'd seen last night, and kids were already out sliding, creating new patterns in the snow.

"You didn't cordon off the area?" she asked.

"What? The whole hill along the road? No, we didn't. As I said, we looked last night and didn't find anything. Where did you see this body?"

She scanned the top of the hill, trying to remember exactly where she'd been standing. She walked forward a few yards and then back again. Crample watched her while stamping his feet and jingling the coins in his pants pocket.

"About here, right below the back of the railroad station," she said.

"Look out!" two boys yelled as they hurtled toward Crample.

He jumped aside. "You kids watch where you're going," he yelled.

They mumbled apologies in his direction and dragged their sled away to find a new sliding spot farther down the hill.

"If you ask me, you probably saw someone who got drunk, fell down the hill, and was temporarily stunned. When she came to, she got up and walked away," Crample said.

"No, I'm sure she was dead."

"How do you know? Have you seen a lot of dead bodies?" He sounded irritated.

"Well, no," she said.

"Let's get out of here." He turned and started to walk back toward the car.

Beth reluctantly followed him. She wanted to investigate further, but her feet were turning into blocks of ice. She decided to come back later, after she got her winter clothes.

Crample dropped Beth off in front of her duplex. The phone was ringing when Beth walked in. She rushed to the kitchen and picked up the receiver of the phone that was mounted on the wall next to a calendar.

"Hello?"

"Oh, hi Sweetie." It was her dad. "You sound out of breath. Were you running?"

"Hi, Dad. No, I just…Never mind. I'll tell you later. What's up?"

"I heard you were talking to the police. They said you found a body. What's going on?"

"Who said that? When did you hear that?"

"At the drugstore when I went to pick up the Sunday paper. You know I always do that. Mrs. Schuman heard it from one of her boys, who heard it from one of the Daniels boys."

"Oh, sure, Bobby Daniels was in the library yesterday. Boy, news travels fast around here."

"So, is it true that you found a body?"

Beth decided to go with the official version. There was no point in alarming her parents and spreading more rumors. "I was probably imagining things. You know me and my crazy imagination. Officer Crample was just here asking some follow-up questions. They checked it out and didn't find a body. He thinks someone slipped, fell down the hill, was momentarily stunned, and then got up and walked away."

"Crample. I could tell you a thing or two about the Cramples," he said.

"Maybe later, Dad. I have to go. I need to take care of some stuff," she said.

"Sure, sure. Anyway, that's not why I called. I wanted to know if we should swing by and pick you up on our way to eleven o'clock mass."

Beth suppressed a bubble of irritation, and the urge to say she was quite capable of making her way to church. But, she remembered how cold it was. A ride would be nice.

"Sure, okay."

"See you soon, Sweetie."

"Dad, wait."

"What is it?"

"Can you bring me my winter coat, boots, and stuff? I've been freezing for the last few days. Ever since it turned so cold."

"Well, I don't know if I can find—"

"Ask Mom. She knows where all my stuff is."

After she hung up, Beth decided it was time for a nice hot bath and breakfast. But first, she would call Evie and ask her to come over this afternoon. They had some investigating to do.

Chapter 3

That Sunday afternoon, Evie sat at Beth's kitchen table eating cookies and drinking tea as she listened to Beth recount her recent experiences. She bit off the head of a Santa-shaped cookie, and then brushed the crumbs off her Nordic-design wool sweater.

"Your mom makes the best cookies," Evie said between bites.

Chestnut rubbed up against Evie's legs. She reached down and petted him absentmindedly. She'd rescued him when he was a kitten, and given him to Beth as a housewarming gift. Beth had always wanted a pet but hadn't had one until then. Her mom didn't let animals into the house. Then, when she was an undergrad, her dorm room didn't allow pets. And later, her ex-boyfriend, Ernie, was allergic to cats. Chestnut remembered Evie and greeted her happily whenever she visited. Cupping her hands around a mug of tea, she leaned back and listened as Beth finished her story.

"...and the cops didn't even keep the kids off the hill, so any discernable path has been destroyed," Beth said. "Crample decided it was probably someone who was temporarily stunned when she fell down the hill and when she came to, she got up and walked away. Not likely. But, we need to prove it. The problem is, there's no body. Maybe we can find a clue at the top of the hill."

Beth and Evie had been best friends since first grade, and Beth knew Evie loved nothing more than a mystery. Together, they read their way through Nancy Drew, Hardy Boys, Sherlock Holmes, and Agatha Christie's stories. Evie's blue eyes sparkled and dimples appeared in her cheeks as she smiled. Beth was happy to see her friend smiling again. Evie had been down ever since her boyfriend, Jim Vincent, had joined the army and had been sent away to basic training. She knew Evie worried he'd be sent to Vietnam.

"Sounds like a plan," Evie said. "We can't count on the local coppers. They're thicker than rice pudding. But what do you think happened?"

"I'm guessing she was dead before she was thrown down the hill. Anyway, she sure looked dead to me. The fall may have killed her, but that seems unlikely. You know that hill. Kids slide down it every day. It's steep, but not so steep it would kill you if you fell wrong. I think she was murdered. I think I saw someone on top of the hill."

"No kidding? But if that happened, where's the body?"

"Maybe the killer spotted me and got nervous because he thought he'd been seen. It would have been easy enough to drive there, load her into a car or truck, and find another dumping spot."

"I suppose so. But, where?"

Beth paused to think while stirring another spoonful of sugar into her tea. "Could be in the woods by the river, dumped in a ditch, or a shed somewhere." She tried to think of any other possibilities. The river was frozen solid. Soon, snowmobilers would be racing up and down it day and night, so that was out. "She could be anywhere. We might have to search for her. But let's start by checking out the top of that hill, first."

"Agreed," Evie said as she reached into the Tupperware container for another cookie. "Sounds like the game is afoot."

Shortly before 4:00 p.m., after they'd polished off the cookies, they bundled up and headed out. As they approached the railroad track, Beth pointed toward the station and said, "You go that way and I'll head down the hill and walk along the bottom of it, like I did last night. I'll yell when you're in the right spot. Okay?"

As she talked, her breath made a cloud of water vapor in the cold air and crystalized on the wool scarf she'd wrapped around her neck. She was glad her mom and dad had rounded up and delivered her winter clothes that morning. Now, she was prepared for the weather.

"Sure thing, Holmes." Evie grinned and turned, flipped her long, blond hair over her shoulder, and walked briskly in the direction that Beth had indicated. Evie was a strapping girl of Nordic descent and nearly six feet tall. Beth hurried down the hill, clumping along as fast as she could in her Sorel boots, on her shorter legs, to keep up with her taller friend. Soon, she was walking along the lower road, dodging kids sliding down the hill, while motioning and calling out to Evie.

"Back, in that direction," she called and waved.

Evie backed up. "About here?" she called out.

"No, not that far." Beth motioned for her to come back. After a few more adjustments, Beth called out, "Yes, right about there. Stay there, okay?"

"Okay," Evie called back.

Beth scrambled up the hill on a footpath trodden in the snow by kids pulling their sleds up the hill. When she got to the top, Evie was bent over, searching in the snow.

"I thought I saw something here," Evie said.

Beth joined her as quickly as she could, lifting each leg high as she forged a path through the snowdrifts, breathing heavily from the exertion. "What? What did you see?"

"I don't know. Something shiny, I think."

"Really? I'll help you look. But wait a sec." Beth held up a hand, turned, and looked around. "Before we move around anymore, check out the patterns in the snow. Do you see that faint path?" She pointed to a slight depression in the snow leading from the railroad track. "It looks like someone came this way."

"You're right. They might have walked to this exact spot," Evie said, and then turned and pointed. "And then to the top of the hill. The snow has drifted in, but this could be the path taken by the killer."

They looked at each other; their eyes opened wide in amazement.

"Come on," Evie said. "Let's look for that shiny object before it starts to get dark."

They both knelt and began sifting through the snow, a handful at a time. Soon, Evie retrieved a small, metal object and held it out to Beth in a wool-mittened hand. The fading rays of the sun glinted off its surface. "Look."

"Wow." Beth slipped off a glove and picked it up, brushed away the snow, and held it up for a look. "It's a silver ring, with some sort of design on it." She turned it around, squinting at it. "It's pretty big—so probably a man's ring. Let's take it back to my place and have a good look at it."

Back in Beth's apartment, they kicked off their boots, threw their coats, hats, scarves, mittens, and gloves into a pile on the couch, and returned to the kitchen. Beth turned on the overhead light, put the ring in the middle of the table between them, and they bent over it for a better look.

Evie picked it up and turned it over in her fingers. "The design is kind of weird. Two snakes, and some other stuff, I think. Have you ever seen one like it?" she said and handed it to Beth.

"No," Beth said. "Do you think it might be a class ring?"

"Could be, I suppose. But I've never seen one like this. Maybe it's some sort of club ring, like the Masons, or something," Evie said as she examined it. "But theirs has a square and compass, doesn't it? Get me some paper, and I'll sketch it."

"Sketch it? Why?" Beth asked.

"So we'll have a record of how it looks. It's a clue. We have to turn it over to the cops. Don't we?"

"I suppose so," Beth said, slowly. "But I don't know why. As far as they are concerned, no crime has been committed, so no clues are needed. They'll toss it into the lost and found box, and it'll probably never be seen again."

"Once the body is found, they'll take it more seriously. They'll go back and take a closer look," Evie said.

"I guess you're right. Okay, I'll drop it off tomorrow," Beth said. She went to find a pencil and paper and returned a short time later carrying a spiral-bound notebook and a pencil.

"Sorry, I don't have any art supplies. Will this do?"

Evie laughed. "Sure. But, I'll have to bring some better stuff over before we find our next clue."

She ripped a page out from the back of the notebook and started to sketch a picture of the ring.

Beth filled the whistling teapot with water and was about to put it on the stove to make cocoa when the phone rang. She grabbed the receiver from the cradle.

"Hello."

"Hello. This is Mrs. Frost," a frantic-sounding, nasal voice on the other end of the line said. "Is this Beth Williams?"

"Yes, this is me," Beth said with hesitation, wondering why the doctor's wife was calling her.

"Oh, good, I'm glad I got hold of you. It's a bit of an emergency."

Beth sucked in a quick breath. Had someone in her family gotten sick or been in an accident? It would be just like her dad to fall off the roof while trying to adjust the TV antenna or something. Evie stopped sketching and watched Beth.

Mrs. Frost continued, "It's regarding the Library Supporters' Appreciation event, which will be held at my house tonight. My high-school-age helpers just phoned to inform me they are ill and won't be able to come. I was hoping you could step in."

Beth sighed with relief. Mrs. and Dr. Frost, who lived up the hill from her parents, were involved in almost every cultural improvement event that happened in Davison City.

"I'm sorry to spring this on you at the last minute, and I understand if you are not available." Mrs. Frost sounded apologetic, seeming to misinterpret the sigh as one of exasperation. "Miss Tanner gave me your name and number. She'll be here, too, as our featured speaker."

"Oh, that's quite all right," Beth said. "I was surprised, that's all. What time do you need me?" She shook her head and waved at Evie, trying to indicate it was nothing for her to worry about.

"Would 7:00 p.m. work for you? It's just a punch and cookies kind of thing. I need someone to pour punch and help with the dishes. The invitation said 7:00 to 9:00. You can bring a friend if one is available. That would make it easier and more enjoyable for you."

"Hold on, my friend, Evie, is here. I'll ask her."

Beth put a hand over the receiver and whispered. "It's Mrs. Frost, the doctor's wife. She's holding some kind of a library supporters' event—punch and cookies—at her house tonight and is looking for help. I suppose you have better things to do."

"Nope, not really. Its sandwiches and popcorn in front of the TV on Sunday nights at our house. Count me in."

Beth gave her the thumbs up, and Evie went back to sketching while Beth finished her phone conversation with Mrs. Frost.

Chapter 4

Beth and Evie stood behind the folding table that they'd set up in the corner of Mrs. Frost's spacious living room, refilling punch glasses with ruby-red punch. After Beth's phone conversation with Mrs. Frost, she and Evie had discussed what to wear and decided on black—it was a sophisticated color. Evie had gone home to change and now she looked elegant in a black A-line dress with white collar and cuffs, nylons, and pumps. Beth didn't have any intact nylons, so she wore black bell-bottom pants, a white shirt with a wide collar and puffy sleeves, which she'd hastily ironed for the occasion, and her penny loafers, which were still a bit damp from walking in the snow last night. Unfortunately, while she ironed her shirt, Chestnut had decided that a warm pair of newly ironed pants made a comfortable perch. Beth hadn't had time to hunt for a lint brush. She hoped no one noticed.

The table was covered with a white tablecloth and laden with a cut-glass punch bowl and punch glasses, small china plates, and large platters of cookies, petit fours, crackers and cheese, grapes, and other nibbles. So far, no one had spilled a drop of the red liquid on Mrs. Frost's white carpet, and Beth focused on making sure she wasn't the first one to do so.

Mrs. Frost had assembled a dozen of Davison City's leading citizens. All in their Sunday best. The men wore suits, the women knee-length polyester blend dresses in a variety of bright-colored patterns. Except for Miss Tanner, who looked business-like in one of her Chanel-inspired tweed suits.

In addition to Mrs. and Dr. Frost, the guests included Miss Tanner, who was talking to Mr. Flack, the newspaper editor, and his wife. Father McClure, from Our Lady of Sorrows Church, was in full story-telling mode. He had cornered the banker, Mr. Brown, the lawyer, Mr. Nobis, Esq. and his wife, and the jewelry store owners, Mr. and Mrs. Gloor.

"I'm going to take a couple of these platters into the kitchen and refill them," Evie said, picking up the cookie and cheese and cracker trays. "This crowd is ravenous. I bet lots of these people skipped dinner and are making a meal out of it." She winked and grinned at Beth, who smiled back.

As Evie disappeared into the kitchen, Mr. Nobis, with an unnaturally tanned complexion and careful comb-over, appeared in front of Beth holding out a punch glass in each hand. "I wonder if you'd be so kind as to refill these for me and my wife, Miss ah, ah..." he stammered.

"Miss Williams. Beth Williams," she said. "I work in the library."

"Oh yes, Miss Williams." His eyes lit up with interest, and he studied her while she refilled the punch glasses. "I heard the most extraordinary thing about you. Didn't you find a body in the park last night?"

Her hand shook a bit as she handed him back the second cup of punch, and she spilled a drop of red liquid on the white shirt cuff that peeked out from under his pinstriped jacket sleeve.

"Oh, I'm so sorry," she said, blushing.

"Not at all. My fault. I distracted you."

He carefully placed the cups down on the table, fished a snowy white handkerchief out of his pants pocket, and dabbed at the stain. His hands were tanned and manicured, and there was a lighter stripe on one finger of his right hand. He must have recently gotten back from a tropical vacation. *Must be nice,* she thought, as her mind wandered to visions of palm trees and white sand beaches that she'd only seen in magazines.

"So, is there any truth to the rumor?" he persisted.

"What? No," she said, jolted back to reality. "I...I caught a glimpse of something. It must have been someone falling down the hill in the park. I jumped to conclusions and reported it to the police. I must've read too many murder mysteries," she said with an embarrassed laugh. "But, whoever it was must have been okay, because there was no one there when Officer Crample went to investigate."

"So, you didn't recognize her, this person?" Mr. Nobis asked.

Before Beth had a chance to answer, Mrs. Nobis, who had been watching them out of the corner of her eye from across the room, while seeming to listen to Father McClure with a fixed smile while playing with her pearl necklace, excused herself, marched over and, after a nod and stiff smile to Beth, turned and said to her husband, "What on earth is taking you so long, Frederick? I could perish from thirst waiting for you to return with the punch. Which one is mine?"

"I'm sorry, dear." He handed his wife one of the glasses of punch. "I was talking to Miss Williams, who works at the library."

"Oh, yes," Mrs. Nobis glanced in Beth's general direction. "I think I've seen her there. Very gratifying work, I'm sure. Come along, Frederick. Miss Tanner is about to speak." She turned and marched off with Mr. Nobis trailing behind her.

Soon, all the guests were finding places on the sofa, matching side chairs, and folding chairs that had been set up for the occasion. Mrs. Gloor sat on the edge of the beige couch, scanning the room. Her eyes narrowed and her lips thinned when she saw Evie emerge from the kitchen carrying a laden cheese and cracker tray, followed by the shorter Mr. Gloor, wearing the same obsequious smile he wore while serving customers, carrying the cookie platter. They deposited their trays on the serving table and Evie thanked him for his help.

"Glad to be of assistance. I was just passing through the room," he said and hurried to take a seat next to his wife.

Evie whispered to Beth. "He said something kind of interesting. I'll tell you about it later."

Miss Tanner began to speak. She thanked everyone for coming and for their continuing support for the library and described some recent acquisitions. In closing, she explained the renovations that would keep the library closed for the next two weeks.

"As many of you know, the current configuration of the library's circulation desk is fixed by architectural details and places it directly in line with the main entrance door. This means that, while seated there, one is blasted with cold air in the winter and hot humid air in the summer.

"We have long desired to add a vestibule or foyer, with a second interior door. Now, thanks to your generosity, as well as a state grant that we have received, that design flaw is about to be remedied. The plans have been finalized and the remodeling will soon begin. Since Christmas and New Year's Day fall mid-week this year, it seemed like a propitious time to close the library for a couple of weeks as the work on the entrance area takes place. We will be open again on January 6th and I look forward to seeing all of you at the library at that time. Thank you."

After polite applause and a few questions, the guests returned to the serving table for the last few nibbles and more punch. Once Mrs. Frost had diplomatically steered the last lingering guest out of the house, the girls went to work collecting plates and glasses, carrying things into the kitchen, folding up the table and chairs, and putting the house back in order.

As they washed dishes in the kitchen, Beth asked, "What was that you were saying about Mr. Gloor? What did he tell you?"

Evie looked around to be sure she wasn't overheard, then said in a low voice, "He said Father McClure was late for the

4:30 mass on Saturday night, and he arrived flushed and out of breath."

"Really? That is odd. I've never known him to be late for mass," Beth whispered.

Mrs. Frost walked into the kitchen. "I can finish up here. You ladies have done enough."

She offered to pay them, which they politely declined. She pressed bags of goodies on them, which they accepted, and they left shortly after 10:00, with her thanks echoing in their ears.

"Come on," Evie said. "I'll give you a ride back to your place."

"Thanks. It's been a long day. I'm so tired; I can barely keep my eyes open."

"Say, when is that brother of yours going to finish fixing your car?"

"Gary promised to have it done before winter quarter starts. He'd better. But, I guess I can't complain since he's doing the work free, and I only pay for parts. Paying customers have to come first. It's nice to have a brother in the auto repair business."

"I'll say. Too bad he doesn't extend that deal to friends of the family. But, I suppose his wife would have a conniption fit if he did."

"Debbie? Yeah, she would. She's already not too thrilled with Gary spending his time doing free work for his family. I get it; they're starting out and need all the money he can earn.

As soon as I finish my degree and get a real job, I'll get a new car, and then I won't need to try to keep that heap going."

Within minutes, they pulled up in front of Beth's place.

"Come over tomorrow morning. We'll compare notes and plan our next step. I'd invite you in, but I'm pooped," Beth said and yawned.

"Okay. What time tomorrow?" Evie asked.

"Not too early—maybe around nine or ten. I want to sleep in since I was rousted out of bed early this morning."

"Sounds good. I'll call you and make sure you're up before I come," Evie said.

Holding her bag of goodies, Beth got out of the car and waved goodbye. She got her key out of her purse and began to unlock the door, but discovered it was already unlocked. *Did I forget to lock it, again?* She wondered.

They'd seldom locked the door at home while she was growing up since someone was usually there and they were always coming and going. Of course, things were different in the cities, where she'd lived in a small apartment and worked, while Ernie went to medical school and then did his residency. But, now that she was back in her hometown, old habits returned and she sometimes forgot to lock up when she went out.

A little uneasy, once inside Beth carefully locked the door behind her before removing her winter wraps and hanging her jacket on a hook behind the door. But, the sight of Chestnut curled up on the chair was reassuring. He opened one eye, looked at her sleepily, yawned, and fell back asleep.

Beth went to the kitchen and dropped her package of goodies on the kitchen table. *It'll keep until morning,* she thought. She was too tired to worry about sorting it out and putting everything away. Then, she returned to the living room, turned on the TV, plopped down on the sofa, and curled up under an afghan that her grandma had knitted. Chestnut stretched and came over and laid on top of her, purring. She nodded off as Walter Cronkite announced, "And that's the way it is," at the end of the news broadcast. When she awoke a couple of hours later to a test pattern and static, she clicked off the TV and went to bed, with Chestnut following her.

Chapter 5

Monday morning, Beth got up early and dressed in jeans, a sweatshirt, and wool socks. She stood at the stove stirring a small pot of oatmeal and heating water for instant coffee when someone knocked on the door.

"Come in. The door's open," she called out. She'd already unlocked it.

Over the counter, which separated the kitchen and living room, she watched Evie enter, followed by a gust of cold air.

"Hi, Beth. You're up early," Evie said. "And it's not even a workday. I guess you'll get a couple of weeks off since the library is closed." She stomped the snow off her boots, unzipped and stepped out of them, and left them on the entry rug.

"No, just a few days—until after Christmas. Then I'll be doing shelf reading and dusting."

"What's shelf reading?" Evie asked as she took off her wraps and flung them on the couch.

"You know, reading call numbers and making sure the books are in order. It's boring. But, I can't afford to be without a paycheck for two weeks, so I'm happy to do it. I'm making coffee and oatmeal. Do you want any?"

"Coffee, yes. Oatmeal, no. I don't know how you can eat that stuff." Evie joined Beth in the kitchen.

Chestnut looked up from his bowl of dry cat food, meowed once in greeting, and went back to crunching his way through his meal.

"You don't know what you're missing. It's good if you put enough stuff in it," Beth said as she stirred brown sugar, cinnamon, and raisins into the pot of oatmeal. She went to the cupboard to get a bowl and spoon, turned, and asked, "Are you sure you don't want some?"

"No thanks, I already ate." Evie put a sketchpad and a bag of pencils on the kitchen table and sat down. "I have an idea."

"What's that?" Beth asked. The teakettle whistled. She took it off the stove, poured two mugs full of hot water, and put them in the middle of the table along with a jar of instant coffee, a sugar bowl, a carton of milk from the fridge, and two teaspoons.

"If you describe the dead girl you saw, I'll sketch her. I brought a sketchpad and colored pencils. Then, we can show her picture to people and see if anyone recognizes her. You know, I hate to keep calling her the dead girl."

"Hmm, I know what you mean. How about we call her Jane Doe?" Beth said.

"That's better. Anyway, so I can sketch Jane Doe and do a better sketch of that ring, too. Where is it?"

"It's on the table, isn't it?" Beth said. She lifted the bag of goodies she'd put there the previous night, looked under it, and moved it to the kitchen counter, but the ring wasn't there. "I thought I left it here." She looked under the table, in case it had rolled off, but it wasn't there, either. "My door was unlocked when I got home last night. I thought I'd forgotten to lock it. You don't suppose someone came in while I was out and took the ring?"

"Hang on," Evie said. "Where's your mom's cookie container? Wasn't that on the table, too? Or did you put it somewhere else?"

"No, it should be here." Puzzled, Beth looked around the kitchen. "Oh, I know," she said, with an exasperated sigh, "I bet my mom sent my dad or sister over to pick it up. She uses it all the time. It's her favorite because it has a carrying handle. Maybe they saw the ring and took that, too, for some reason. If it was my dad, maybe he knows who it belongs to and wants to return it to them. If it was my sister, she probably thought it was cool looking and borrowed it. Honestly, I wish they'd left a note. I'm starting to regret giving them a spare key."

"Yeah, that's probably what happened. After all, who would break into a place and steal a Tupperware container?" Evie said with a laugh.

"I'll call home after breakfast and find out," Beth said.

Evie opened her sketchpad and got out a pencil. "Now, describe the dead girl, I mean, Jane."

"Okay, but remember, I only had one quick look."

"I know, but you have an amazing memory for faces."

"Well, I don't know about that. Let's see. She was blond and thin, with long hair." Beth gazed out the kitchen window and stared at the slate-gray sky, beyond the bare branches of the elm tree in the back yard, as she visualized her. "She was wearing a long, dark skirt—black or navy—and a long, dark coat. It seemed like a lot of clothing. At first, I thought it was a bundle of clothes. It wasn't until I got closer and I saw arms and legs that I wondered if it was a person. Then I touched her, she turned over, and I saw her face." Beth shuddered. "Her eyes were wide open, blank, and staring."

"What color were they?"

"Blue, I think, and she was wearing a lot of dark eye shadow."

"What was the shape of her face? Long and thin, or small and round?"

"Sort of thin."

Beth continued to describe her and Evie sketched, asking questions, and making changes as needed—the nose a little smaller, the lips fuller, and the forehead lower. Suddenly, Chestnut jumped up onto the table and attacked Evie's pencil.

"No, Chestnut, get down," Beth said and put him back on the floor.

Evie laughed. "Poor kitty. He wants to help." She went back to sketching.

After further revisions, Beth said, "Yes, that's an amazing likeness. Someone who knows her will certainly recognize her from your sketch. You're such a good artist."

"Thanks. I do seem to have a knack for it, don't I? Maybe I should be a police sketch artist."

"Or, maybe your drawings will be hanging in the Louvre one day."

"Yeah, right. So, who do you think we should show this to? We have to be careful it's not the wrong person. We don't want word getting around that we can ID the victim."

"True. And I don't want my parents to know I saw an actual dead girl until we're 100% sure," Beth said. "I told my dad Crample's theory, and I'm pretending that I think he's right. You know how my mom gets—all nervous and worried."

"Yeah, I know. So, it should be someone who knows a lot of people, but who can keep their mouth shut about it. Any ideas?" Evie said.

"I have a few people in mind. Just a sec, let me call home and find out what happened last night, and then we'll get going," Beth said.

Beth called and talked to her dad. After hanging up, she said, "As I thought, it was my sister who came over last night. She got her driver's license recently, and loves to run errands if it means a chance to drive. But, she's not home now. I'll get it back from her later. Meanwhile, we can do a little investigating and shopping."

"Okay, but only until three o'clock. I promised my mom I'd help her. She invited some people for Christmas, so she's going nuts with the cooking and cleaning."

"Sounds like my mom. It'll just be us this year, but I still need to help her tomorrow. After today, we'll put things on hold until after Christmas. We don't need to go to the police station to drop off the ring, so that'll save some time. I need to get one more gift. Something for my sister. It's impossible to find something a 16-year-old girl likes. Do you have any suggestions?"

"Hmm," Evie paused. "How about jewelry? Here's a thought, we can go to the jewelry store and look at something for Cathy, and we can ask Mr. Gloor some questions, too. Two birds, etc."

"That's a good idea. We could say we want a ring for a man, like the one we found, and describe it. Maybe it even came from his shop. Do you have the sketch with you?"

"Yup, it's in my bag," Evie said, patting her purse.

"Or, maybe we shouldn't show it to him. Do you think we should keep that a secret, for now?"

"I'm not sure." Evie bit her lower lip. "How about we start by asking him about rings in general. And let me do most of the talking."

"Sure, but why?"

"I think he has a little thing for me?"

"Really?" Beth laughed. "Why do you think that?"

"The way he acted in the kitchen at the Frost's house. He was all weird and smarmy."

"No kidding? What an old letch. No wonder his wife watches him like a hawk," Beth said. "But wait, she'll be there, too. Unless we catch him when she goes to lunch. Let's walk by the store around noon and see if he's there alone. Meanwhile, let's pop in at my brother's auto repair shop. He knows a lot of people. Nearly everyone in town has had their car worked on there at one time or another. He might recognize our Jane Doe. And maybe I can get an ETA on my car repairs."

Evie and Beth drove through downtown to Dave's Auto Repairs, located on the south end of Main Street, where gas stations and tire shops mixed with houses needing paint. Dave had been the original owner and, some thirty years later, even though the store had changed hands several times, it still bore his name. They parked in the gravel parking lot and walked across potholes filled with ice and hard-packed snow. Beth noticed her car was still parked where she'd left it a week ago, so she didn't have much hope it had been worked on.

The bell on the door jangled as they went in, and the door slammed shut behind them. Inside, the air was redolent with motor oil. To their left, two vinyl chairs and a battered end table, piled high with tattered issues of *Car and Driver* magazine, formed a waiting area for customers. In front of them was an ancient metal desk. Behind it, leaning back in a rolling chair, his oil-streaked boots propped up on the desk, was Sam, one of Gary's motor-head buddies. He was flipping through an issue of the magazine, holding it in hands blackened with oil that outlined his fingernails. He was about Beth and Evie's age, but from what Gary told Beth, he acted more like an overaged teenager, only working part-time and living at home with his parents.

"Oh, hi there," he said. He lowered his feet to the floor and regarded them with a smile that Beth supposed he thought was charming. "What can I do for you girls?"

"Hi, Sam. Is Gary here?" Beth said.

"Oh, hi Beth. I heard you moved back home from the Twin Cities. And you're Evie Hanson, right?"

Evie nodded and said, "Hi, Sam."

"Yup, I'm back," Beth said. "I'm taking some classes at North Dakota State."

"Well, welcome home. As for Gary, he's out."

"When do you expect him back?"

"Don't know, exactly. Maybe a couple of hours. He went somewhere with the missus—Christmas shopping, I suppose. I'm holding down the fort. Anything I can help you with?"

"You don't know if he's gotten to my car yet, do you?"

"Nope—don't know. Sorry," he said again. "But I'll tell him you stopped by."

"Okay, thanks. And Merry Christmas," she said. They waved as they left.

After the door closed behind them, Evie made a disgusted face and said, "He knows perfectly well who I am."

"That's right; you went out with him a few times in high school, didn't you?"

"Unfortunately, yes. But it didn't take too long to figure out I didn't like him."

"He was always eyeing other girls, as I recall."

"Yeah, a real loser."

Beth laughed. "I'd say you dodged a bullet. He only works for my brother occasionally, doesn't have a steady job, and still lives with his mom."

Back in the car, Beth said, "That didn't take long. We have some time to kill before we can go over to the jewelry store. One person I thought we could talk to is Father McClure. Do you want to go see him now? Maybe he can give us a lead. He knows nearly everyone in town. I suppose we can trust his discretion."

"Good idea. But, we can't barge in and start asking him questions. What's our cover story?" Evie asked.

"I have a plan. We'll say a friend of ours is thinking about becoming a Catholic."

"Won't he ask who it is?"

"Yeah, I suppose so." Beth paused, then said, "How about this—we say this friend isn't quite sure yet, so they want to remain anonymous for the time being."

"That sounds perfect. You do have a devious mind," Evie said.

"Thanks. I think," Beth said.

Father McClure's housekeeper, Mrs. Karpova, opened the door of the rectory. She was a small woman with tightly curled, short, gray hair. She wore a flowered bib apron over a housedress and held a duster in one hand.

"We'd like to see Father McClure," Beth said.

"Do you have an appointment?" she asked as she looked them up and down, seeming to search for something to disapprove of.

"No, but we hoped he might have a few minutes to talk to us," Beth replied. "We are—"

She cut Beth off. "I know who you are," she said, and reluctantly opened the door to let them in. She left them standing on the entry mat while she disappeared down the hall to check with the Father and returned a few moments later.

"He said he'll see you. Take your boots off. I just vacuumed the floor."

They quickly followed her instructions and followed her as she hurried down the hall and led them into the study.

Father McClure stood up behind the desk. "So nice to see both of you. Please, won't you take a seat?" He gestured toward the two chairs facing the desk.

"Don't let these girls take up too much of your time," Mrs. Karpova sniffed. "You have sermons to write."

"That's quite all right," he said, with a dismissive wave in her direction. "Won't you bring us some coffee and cookies, Mrs. Karpova? I'm sure the girls would—"

"Yes, yes," she cut him off mid-sentence. "It's not as if I don't have enough..." the rest of her complaint was muffled as she closed the door, with unnecessary firmness, behind her.

"I'm sorry. Is this a bad time?" Beth asked.

"No, no, not at all," Father McClure's said. His eyebrows raised in surprise.

Beth surmised he was so used to Mrs. Karpova's manner that he'd ceased to notice it. She continued, "Evie and I were out shopping and, when we passed by, we decided to stop and ask about instructions for a friend of ours."

"Instructions? Oh, you mean religious instructions?"

"Yes, you see she's thinking of becoming a Catholic and we thought we'd get some information for her, as far as what that would entail. Right, Evie?"

"Oh, yes. That's right," Evie said as two spots of color rose in her cheeks. Beth could see she wasn't at all comfortable lying to a priest.

Fortunately, Father McClure didn't seem to notice. For some reason, that brief exchange reminded him of the time a cow got into the cemetery, and he was well into reciting this oft-told tale when Mrs. Karpova rattled in with a tray containing three cups of coffee and a plate of cookies, slammed it down on his desk, sloshing a bit of coffee into the saucers, and hustled back out, again.

Beth and Evie sat back and enjoyed the excellent coffee and cookies, smiled, and nodded while he rambled on. The cookies were gone by the time he wound up the story.

"...and we didn't need any fertilizer to keep the grass green that year," he said, and looked around, as if for applause.

On cue, both Evie and Beth laughed politely.

"So, you were saying. A friend of yours wants religious instruction? Who is she?"

Beth said, "She isn't sure. There are family complications. So, she prefers to remain anonymous, for the time being."

"Of course. Families can be complicated, yes, yes."

"We're just gathering information. I suppose she would come here for instruction. What times would be good?" Beth said.

"How about Saturday afternoons? Evie said. "Because she works during the week."

"Oh, yes. I think that could be arranged," Father McClure said blandly. "I think I have some literature here." He started to root through the drawers of his desk. "But, not too late because I have to be ready for Saturday evening mass."

"Of course," Evie said. "You wouldn't want to be late for mass."

"No, no I wouldn't..." he paused and his eyes narrowed as he looked at Evie more closely. The red spots in her cheeks had spread.

"Anyway," Beth interrupted. "We'll tell her to call and arrange it with you, shall we?"

"Yes, that would be best."

"Well, we don't want to take up any more of your time," Beth said. He stood and handed Beth a brochure entitled, "So, You Are Thinking of Becoming a Catholic."

Beth and Evie stood, too. Beth said to Evie, "Didn't you also want to show Father that sketch of the missing girl?"

"Oh, yes. We're showing it to everyone," Evie said as she got it out of her bag.

"A missing girl? I hadn't heard of a missing girl," he said.

Evie handed him her sketch. As he looked at it, the color drained from his face and he seemed momentarily frozen.

"Where did you get this?" he asked.

"I drew it," Evie said. "Beth saw this girl fall down the hill in the park. She described her, and I sketched her from the description."

"Oh, yes. I heard something about your experience." He nodded to Beth. "When was it? Saturday evening, I think. Someone said you found a body. Is that right?"

"No, that was a misunderstanding. She must have been stunned because she was gone by the time the police got there,"

Beth said. "But Evie and I don't recognize her, and she seems to have disappeared. We're trying to figure out who she is so we can check and see if she's all right. Do you recognize her?"

He stared at the picture for another long moment, and then said, "No, no I don't know her. Now, if there's nothing else, I should get back to work." He handed the sketch back to Evie, sat down, and started shuffling the papers on his desk.

They said goodbye and left.

"Wow, that was weird," Evie said. Once they were outside.

Chapter 6

Beth and Evie parked across the street from Gloor's Jewelry Store and waited for Mrs. Gloor to leave for lunch. Evie fiddled with the tuning knob, searching for a station playing something other than Christmas music.

"If I hear 'White Christmas' one more time, I'm going to snap." She found a Top-100 station broadcasting from Grand Bend, North Dakota. "Finally, something good," she said as she cranked up the volume. Then, she leaned back, tapped her toes, and hummed, out of tune, along with, 'I Heard it Through the Grapevine.'

"Keep it down," Beth said, twisting the volume knob. "We're supposed to be inconspicuous. We're on a stakeout. Remember?"

Evie laughed and reached over to turn the music back up. Beth slapped at her hand, laughing, too. The door to the jewelry store opened.

"Look, there she goes." Beth pointed.

Mrs. Gloor stalked out of the store and down the sidewalk. She was well known to adhere to a strict schedule. Rumor had it that she'd walk out of the store at the stroke of noon, even if that meant customers had to wait for her husband to finish helping other customers, before helping them, rather than put off her lunch break. Scowling and staring straight ahead, she power walked to the corner and then turned right.

"Let's go," Beth said as she snapped off the radio. "But, pretend we're window shopping first. So we can see if he's alone in the store before we go in. Okay?"

"You betcha," Evie said.

The girls scampered across the street, then stopped to gaze into the store's display window. Strategically aimed lights brought out the facets of the glistening stones and precious metals on display, along with some more affordable items such as charm bracelets, religious medals, and small trinkets for curio cabinets. Many of the price tags had been carefully turned face down, so customers would have to go inside to inquire.

"Oh, look," Evie said. "They have some cute charms."

While pretending to admire the wares, Beth scoped out the place. Mr. Gloor was alone. Holding a spray bottle of glass cleaner in one hand and a white cotton rag in the other, he wandered around wiping away fingerprints on the display cases.

"Come on. It's go time," Beth grinned at Evie.

"Remember. Let me do the talking," Evie said before she opened the door.

Beth nodded and followed her in. A welcoming rush of warm air, scented with glass cleaner and air freshener, enveloped them.

Mr. Gloor brightened at the sight of customers and put the glass cleaner and cloth down next to the cash register. His smile got wider, and more genuine when he realized that one of them was Evie. "Hello. How can I help you girls? Evie, isn't it? And, and…"

"Beth," Evie supplied the name, gesturing toward her friend.

Beth didn't mind. She was used to being overlooked while standing next to her taller, better-looking friend. In fact, it was fine. That way, she could watch without being noticed.

"We're doing a little Christmas shopping. Mostly just window shopping," Evie said.

Mr. Gloor laughed as though that were a true witticism. "Well, let me know if there is something in particular you'd like to see."

"How about charms for charm bracelets. Do you have any of those?" Evie said.

"Oh, yes. Those are quite popular with the young ladies. Let me show you."

He eagerly led them to a display case, went behind it, and slid open the glass door. Beth stood a few feet away examining an earring display while watching as Mr. Gloor pulled tiny boxes containing charms out of the case and handed them to Evie. She admired each one in turn, her eyes wide, smiling as she leaned in toward Mr. Gloor when she took them from him, and then placed them down on the counter between them, periodically reaching up to flip her long blond hair back over a shoulder. Beth admired the act. Evie could be quite the flirt.

"What was that you said about Father McClure being late for mass last Saturday? I wonder why. Normally, he's never late," Evie said while admiring a tiny replica of a pocket watch.

"It was odd. That's why it stuck in my mind. Plus the fact that his pants—at least what I could see sticking out from below his cassock—were wet. He only lives across the sidewalk, which is always well shoveled, from the side door of the church. So, I wondered why he would have been walking through deep snow."

"Yes, that is a good question. Perhaps he was called away to a sickbed."

"I suppose so. Perhaps we'll hear. We pray for members of the parish who are sick at each mass, so maybe we'll find out next weekend."

"Or, at Christmas mass."

"Yes, of course."

Beth closely listened to this exchange while she spun the rotating display rack, and pretended to examine the earrings on it.

"Oh, I can't decide," Evie said, turning to Beth, "What do you think?"

Beth came over and scanned the charms in their cute little boxes. A little gold car, still in the case, caught her eye. Perhaps her sister would like that one, to commemorate getting her driver's license. "How much is that one?" she asked.

Mr. Gloor took it out of the case and looked at the tag on the bottom of the box. "It's $3.00."

Beth hesitated. That was about two hours of her wages. She tried to work out how much money she had with her and what else she needed.

Noting her hesitation, Mr. Gloor said, "We're planning an after-Christmas sale and these will be 25% off. So, it would be $2.25. I could let you have the sale price, now, if you girls promise not to tell anyone." He winked and smiled at Evie, and she returned his smile.

"I'll take it," Beth said, feeling good about getting a special deal.

While he rang up Beth's purchase, he asked Evie, "How's your engagement ring working out. No problems, I hope."

Evie tilted her hand to catch the light and admired the small, but sparkly, diamond. "No, no problems. It's still beautiful." Looking meaningfully at Beth, she continued, "Speaking of rings. I was wondering about a particular ring that I saw someone wearing, and I wondered if you might know something about it."

Mr. Gloor turned and handed Beth her change and the package with mumbled thanks and no eye contact, and then turned back to Evie, smiled, and said, "Oh yes? What was it like?"

Beth tried to catch Evie's eye and signal her to not say too much—this was not the plan. But Evie ignored her.

"It was really weird, but kind of groovy, there was an engraving of the figure of some sort of man. At least, I think it was a man. It had a man's body, with snakes for legs, and a rooster's head. I think. I didn't get a really good look at it," Evie said.

Mr. Gloor's smile momentarily froze, but he quickly recovered his composure. "It sounds very odd. As you say, maybe you didn't quite see it correctly. A rooster and a snake? No, I don't think I've ever seen anything like that."

Once they were back in Evie's car, Beth said, "Why did you ask him that? I thought we decided to keep a low profile. Now he knows that we saw that weird ring."

"Yeah, sorry about that, but I had an opening and decided to go for it. If we're going to make any progress on this, we have to start somewhere. Anyway, for all we know, the ring has nothing to do with the case. It could have been there in the snow for ages. That was crazy, though. Did you see his reaction?"

"I sure did. He was lying. He knew exactly what you were describing. So, why would he lie about it?"

"Where to next, Holmes?" Evie asked.

"To the dime store lunch counter for sustenance, I think. Since I got a bargain on the charm, I can afford to blow some cash on a burger and shake. What do you think?"

"Sounds good to me." Evie started the car and off they went.

Chapter 7

Beth and Evie sat across from each other in a booth at the Woolworths lunch counter. Beth had been famished and had splurged on her lunch, spending more on it than she'd saved by getting the discounted price on her sister's Christmas present from Gloor. She'd already polished off a hamburger, fries, and Coke, and now was digging into her dessert—a banana split made with a whole banana, split the long way, that cradled three scoops of ice cream, each one covered by a different topping, and surrounded by a generous portion of whipped cream, with a cherry on top.

Evie cast envious glances as Beth dug into it, while she sampled her dessert—a square of Jell-O topped with a small blob of whipped cream. "I wish I could eat that, too, but if I did, I'd weigh twice as much," she said.

"That's one advantage to not having a boyfriend," Beth said. "After eight years of trying, without much success, to get slim enough to fit in with the wives and girlfriends of Ernie's pals, it's nice to skip the salads and eat what I want."

Evie looked up, opened her mouth as if to say something, and then closed it again.

"What?" Beth asked.

"Nothing, I was just thinking. Don't answer if you don't want to. Do you ever hear from Ernie? Never mind. I shouldn't have brought it up."

"Don't worry about it. No, I haven't heard from him since last summer. Believe me, I'm glad it's over. If I'm lucky, I'll never see him or hear from him again. But, I'm not bitter." Beth said with an ironic chuckle.

"You could do a lot better," Evie said.

"Maybe, but I'll never know because I'm swearing off men. If Ernie and I had stayed together, who knows, I might have gotten married and had kids. But now, I can go to graduate school and see the world before I settle down. Actually, he did me a favor."

Officer Crample strolled up, stopped, and leaned on their table. "Hi, girls. Taking a break from Christmas shopping?"

Beth stopped eating, spoon suspended in midair, and then returned it to her dish. "Oh, hello Officer Crample." It had taken her a second to recognize him out of uniform. Now he was wearing a barn jacket, jeans, and boots. "Do you know my friend Evie Hanson?"

"It's Bill when I'm off duty. Yes, Evie and I have met. How are ya doing?" He nodded in her direction.

"Fine, and you?"

"Good. Mind if I sit? Shopping wears me out." He looked pointedly at Beth, who ignored him and resumed eating her banana split. Evie looked back and forth between the two of them, shrugged, and then slid over as far as she could in the small booth, and he sat down next to her, crowding her into the corner.

"Careful with the sweets, you'll ruin your girlish figure," he said to Beth, pointing at her dessert.

"What's it to you?" Beth said, pulling a face, and then scooping up a large bite and devouring it.

He laughed. "So, has the girl who fell down the hill turned up, yet?"

Beth rested her spoon on the edge of her dish and fixed him with a steely look. "That'd be a trick since she's dead."

He laughed again. "So you say, but no one has reported a missing girl."

A waitress came over and smiled at him. "Can I get something for you, Bill?"

"Just coffee, black. Thanks, Gloria. And put these girls' orders on my bill, too."

Beth and Evie both protested that it wasn't necessary, but he insisted.

After the waitress left, Evie said, "We have a picture of her."

"No, no, don't…" Beth trailed off.

He looked from Beth to Evie. "You have a picture? How did you get a picture?" he asked.

"Well, not a picture—a sketch," Evie said. "Beth described her and I drew it from her description. Should I show it to him?" she asked Beth.

Beth wasn't sure if it was a good idea, or not. He was a cop and he knew a lot of different people—like the waitress, for example. He might be able to identify the girl. Evie's sketch was a very good likeness.

Beth shrugged. "I guess so."

"Do you want to see it?" Evie asked Bill.

"Sure, why not." He smiled, obviously not expecting much.

The waitress returned with a thick, beige mug of coffee, napkin, and spoon, and placed them in front of Bill. He reached across Evie and grabbed the sugar dispenser, dumped three spoonfuls of sugar into his coffee, and stirred it.

"Speaking of avoiding sweets. Maybe you should take your own advice," Beth said, pointing at his coffee cup with her spoon.

"I have to keep up my energy," he said.

Beth snorted derisively.

Meanwhile, Evie dug in her purse, retrieved the sketch, and handed it to Bill. He unfolded it and took a slurp of coffee as he examined it. Beth watched as his eyes narrowed and then opened wide.

"You know her," Beth said.

"Yeah, maybe. It looks like a girl I've seen once or twice. But, as far as I know, she's alive and well." He continued to stare at the sketch for a few more moments and then handed it to Beth. "Maybe I should check it out."

"So, what's her name?" Beth asked.

"She calls herself Crystal Jones. I don't suppose that name means anything to you girls."

They shook their heads, no.

"I figured as much," he said.

"What do you mean 'calls herself'?" Evie asked.

"It means that I'm not sure that's really her name."

Beth and Evie looked at each other with raised eyebrows, then shrugged.

"Okay, so when are you going to check it out?" Beth asked.

"Not today. I'm off duty."

"All right, but can't you call headquarters and have someone else check it out?"

"I could, but what's the rush?"

"What's the rush?" Beth's voice rose. "A girl is dead, maybe murdered, and you ask 'what's the rush?' How about gathering evidence before it's destroyed, for example."

"Shh," Bill said, looking at the waitress who had stopped refilling coffee cups and turned toward them. "Keep your voice down. Okay, I'll look into it today. Happy? Maybe you should come along."

"Me? What for?"

"To make an identification. When we find her alive, which I'm sure we will, you'll see that it's her and give up this murder mystery nonsense."

"Okay, I'm in. How about you, Evie?"

"Sorry. I promised my mom I'd be home by three. Remember?" Evie said.

"Oh, right." Beth looked at the clock over the grill, and then consulted her watch. "It's past two, already? It's later than I thought."

"It's always later than you think it is," Evie said.

"Mind if I keep this?" Beth asked Evie, indicating the sketch.

"No, that's fine."

Beth refolded it and stuck it into her purse. After Bill paid the bill, they gathered their things, bundled up, and headed out.

"Call me later today and tell me what you find out," Evie said.

"I will," Beth promised.

Evie turned toward her car and Bill and Beth headed the other way. He stopped next to a beat-up Ford pickup truck that, under a layer of salt, appeared to be dark green. He unlocked the passenger side door, and held it open for Beth. She climbed in.

He slammed the door shut behind her, and then went around and got in on the driver's side. She kicked aside some oily rags and candy wrappers on the floor to make a spot for her feet.

"Sorry about the mess. I wasn't expecting company," he said.

"Not a problem," she said. She compared his truck, unfavorably, to the vehicles owned by her brother and her dad. They always kept the interiors of their vehicles neat, even if the exterior didn't get washed all winter long. "Where are we headed? Is it far?"

"A little ways—maybe fifteen miles outside of the city limit—toward Grand Bend."

"Okay, so she's not a Davison City girl. Is it even in your jurisdiction?"

"Not normally, but if the accident," he glanced in her direction, "or whatever it was, happened in Davison, it will be."

Within minutes they were outside of the city limits and headed north and then west toward North Dakota. Bill sped along with, what seemed to Beth to be, a reckless disregard for safety, down the thin ribbon of pavement that connected Davison City and Grand Bend. She turned away, trying to ignore him, and hoped for the best as she watched the sun glint at a low angle off of the surrounding, white-blanketed fields. Restless swirls and eddies of blowing snow danced patterns across the highway, its edges uneven with snowdrifts, as the wind unceasingly strove to bury the lonely, two-lane highway. Here and there in the distance, small clumps of scraggly, wind-blown trees—now, bare-branched—attempted to protect farmsteads.

Bill turned on the radio and 'I Saw Mommy Kissing Santa Claus' blared out. After another ten-minute drive, Bill turned right and drove, at a slightly slower pace, down the rough and rutted gravel road, past a few of those farmsteads. The only signs of life were the thin spirals of smoke issuing from the chimneys of the houses. A lone farmer, hunched against the cold wind, stopped on his way back from the barn to look up and notice the passing vehicle.

"I have to warn you, the place we're going…It's not a nice place. Not a place for girls like you."

"Why? What do you mean?"

"You'll see," he said.

Chapter 8

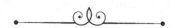

Bill drove for another five minutes without passing another farm, then turned left into a long driveway—poorly plowed and badly rutted—past a screen of evergreen trees, and stopped in front of a dilapidated farmhouse.

"We're here," he said. "Do you want to wait in the truck?"

"No. What good would that do? I can't identify her unless I see her, can I?" Beth said.

"I could bring her out so you could take a look, but suit yourself," he shrugged.

He jumped out and came around to open her door. Before he got there, Beth had already hopped out and was heading toward the house.

"Hold on," he said. "I'll go first."

Bill pounded on the door, then stood on the crumbling doorstep waiting for a few moments, and then pounded again. Standing at the foot of the step, Beth turned her back to the biting wind and stomped her feet to keep warm. A few minutes later, they heard voices and footsteps inside the house. A young man opened the porch door, followed by a rush of warm air redolent with the sickly-sweet, skunky smell that Beth recognized as the same odor that emanated from frat parties. Marijuana. He appeared to be in his mid-twenties, with straggly, brown, shoulder-length hair, and a long mustache. He wore a brightly colored paisley shirt, half unbuttoned to show off the thick gold chain underneath, bell-bottom jeans, and wool socks. One toe was starting to poke out of a hole forming in the sock on his right foot, which he kept propped against the door to keep it partially shut.

"Hi, Allen," Bill said.

"It's Al." He looked past Bill and stared at Beth. "Who's she?" he nodded toward her. His eyes were half shut and his mouth hung open slightly.

Beth thought he would be sort of attractive, in a sleazy way, if he didn't have such a stupid look on his face.

"None of your damn business, Allen," Bill said.

"The name is Al, not Allen."

"Okay, Al," Bill said, stressing and elongating the name. "We're looking for Crystal. Is she here?"

"Who?"

"Your girl, Crystal Jones."

"She's not my girl."

"Whatever. Just bring her out here."

"You don't have any jurisdiction here, Bill. So, beat it." Al started to close the door.

"Jurisdiction or not, bring her out here, or I'll bust up your pretty-boy face." Bill pushed back against the door.

"Back off, asshole. She's not here."

"Where is she?"

"Damned if I know. She took off. Okay?"

"Took off? When was this?"

"Sometime Saturday night. I haven't seen her since."

"Excuse me if I don't take your word for it. Mind if we come in and take a look around?"

"Yes, I mind. Do you have a warrant?"

"I don't need a warrant. This is a social call. So don't worry about flushing your drugs or hiding whatever else you've got going on, I'm just here looking for the girl. Period. If I have to come back, it'll be a different story."

Reluctantly, Al opened the door and gestured for them to come in. He led them through the porch, into the kitchen, and then through floor-length, paisley curtains hanging in the doorway between the rooms, into the living room. There, two girls in their late teens or early twenties, wearing miniskirts and tank tops, lolled on a dilapidated couch smoking hand-rolled joints and staring at the TV as it blasted out *Days of Our Lives*. Incongruously, they wore fluffy slippers on their feet.

The floors must be cold, Beth thought. A red-hot space heater glowed in the corner, rendering the room stuffy, probably so they would be comfortable in their skimpy outfits. She unwrapped her scarf, unzipped her jacket, took off her hat and gloves, and stuffed them into her jacket pockets. The girls didn't move, only their eyes followed Al, Bill, and Beth.

"Her bedroom is upstairs, on the right," Al said. "See for yourselves. She's not here,"

Bill went up, and Beth followed him. Crystal's bedroom was small and cluttered. Pictures of movie stars torn from magazines adorned the cracked, blue-painted walls. Clothing was strewn across her unmade double bed.

"Look for something to ID her," Bill said.

"Like what?"

"Anything—driver's license, letters, address book. Whatever." He started searching through dresser drawers and poking around in the closet. "She left a lot of stuff behind if she took off," he said.

Beth looked over the contents strewn across the top of her dressing table, sitting to the right of the door. There were half-used bottles of perfume and makeup, crumpled tissues, costume jewelry, a St. Michael the Archangel holy card, brushes and combs, and a curling iron. She opened the drawer. It was full of more half-used cosmetics and costume jewelry. She closed the drawer, looked up, and saw, stuck in the edges of the mirror, a few photographs.

Beth felt a chill go down her spine as she recognized the girl staring out of the photos as the one she'd seen, dead, at the bottom of the hill in Central Park. She removed one, a strip of four pictures from a photo booth, of Crystal mugging for the camera. She looked so young, innocent, and happy. The other photo was of Crystal and another girl leaning against a car.

"Hey Bill, take a look at these," she said.

"What?" He came over and stood next to her.

She handed him the strip of pictures. "That's her. That's the girl I saw."

They heard heavy footsteps coming up the stairs, and then Al came into the bedroom. "Find what you're looking for?" he asked.

"Don't know, yet. Mind if I keep these pictures?" Bill asked Al, holding up the strip of photos.

"Keep whatever you want. If you find that chick, tell her I'm dumping her shit into the garbage at the end of the week if she doesn't come back to claim it. When she comes back, and I know she will, I'll set her straight. No more bugging out whenever she feels like it. This is her last chance."

"What do you mean "last chance"? Has she taken off before?"

"Yeah, once or twice, but she always comes back—doesn't have anywhere else to go, I guess. Foster kid who aged out of the system, no friends or family to fall back on, the usual sob story. She doesn't get how good she has it here."

"Right, a real fairyland." Bill folded his arms and rocked back on his heels. "So, when, exactly, was the last time you saw her?"

"I told you, man, Saturday."

"What time?"

"I don't know. Sometime in the afternoon, I guess."

"It looks like she was getting ready for something special," Beth said, indicating the clothes on the bed and the items on the dressing table.

"Yeah, a special party," Al smirked at Beth, looking her up and down. "Say, baby, how'd you like to make some real money? Some guys like them curvy."

"Back off, asshole," Bill said, taking a threatening step towards Al. "Can't you see she's a nice girl?"

"Okay, okay, I get it. She's with you."

"So, Crystal was going to a party," Bill said. "Who with? Where was this party? Did they pick her up, or did you drop her someplace?"

"My girls' dates prefer to remain anonymous," Al said.

"I don't care what the johns prefer. Give me a name."

"I don't have a name."

"How is that possible? How was it arranged and how do you get paid?"

"They send me cash, with details about which girl they want, where, and when. Lately, it was always Crystal. I follow the directions."

"How about a location?"

"I dropped her at the Big Boy restaurant on the edge of town. Okay? And that's all I'm saying. Like I told you, take what you want. On second thought, when you find her, tell her not to come back. I've had it with that bitch." He turned and went back downstairs.

"Asshole," Bill said under his breath. He leaned in to take a closer look at the picture on the edge of the mirror and removed it. "That car might help. I can read part of the license plate number. Maybe I can run down who owns it." He took it and put both of the pictures into the inside pocket of his jacket.

Back in the truck, Beth said, "So they are prostitutes, and he's a, a..."

"Yup, he's their pimp."

"For real? Good, God! I knew that happened in the cities, but I had no idea that kind of thing was going on around here."

"There's probably lots you don't know. And you should be glad about that."

"So, you are going to try to track down the car in the picture? When?"

"I don't know. When I go back to work, I guess."

"Are you convinced that she's dead, now?"

Bill glanced at her and laughed. "No, not really. I believe you saw Crystal on Saturday night. But I have no reason to think she's dead. Far as I'm concerned, she got drunk, fell down the hill, then got up and wandered off—like I said before. You heard Al. She took off before and then came back. Odds are, she'll show up again. Leave it to me. If she doesn't turn up, and I can figure out her identity, I'll try to track her down. Okay?"

Beth mulled this over as they rattled down the gravel road and turned onto the highway, heading back to Davison City. There must be something she could do. Clearly, Bill wasn't taking this seriously. He probably couldn't care less—just like Al—whether Crystal was alive or dead. She wasn't important enough for them to care about. Well, she wasn't going to let it drop. Someone had to care.

"Let me have those pictures from the photo booth."

"No way. You're going to butt in and cause problems."

"No, I won't. Just let me have one to show to Evie. She drew the sketch, and I want to show her how close she came to the actual likeness."

He threw her a skeptical sidelong look, but he dug into his inside jacket pocket with his right hand, while steering with his left, and handed her the strip of pictures.

"Okay, tear one of them off. But don't mess around with this. Think about it, if you did see a dead girl, someone out there is responsible and that someone doesn't want to get caught. You start asking too many questions, and you could be next. Got it?"

Beth carefully folded back the bottom picture and tore it away from the others. "Got it," she said. He was right. She'd have to be careful about who she talked to.

Chapter 9

Beth flopped down on the couch in the basement family room to digest her mother's Christmas Eve dinner of ham, scalloped potatoes, green bean casserole, and pumpkin pie, with all the extras. The piney scent of the Christmas tree that stood in the corner mixed with the baking and cooking smells to create the unique scent of Christmas. The TV set was on and broadcasting the latest news from NASA, and a special Christmas Eve message from space was about to begin.

"Shove over," her sister, Cathy, said to her as she wedged herself between Beth and their brother, Gary. His wife, Debbie, sat on the other end of the couch.

"Say, Cathy, I've been meaning to ask you, did you see a ring on my kitchen table when you came over to pick up Mom's Tupperware container the other day?" Beth asked.

"A ring. What kind of ring?"

"Just a ring I'm looking for. Did you see one?"

"No, I didn't. Why?"

"I misplaced one, that's all."

"And, you wondered if I'd swiped it. Right?" Cathy said and laughed. "No, and don't blame me every time you can't find something. With the piles of books, papers, and other stuff you have laying around, I'm not surprised things go missing. Anyway, since when did you start wearing jewelry?"

Beth's dad was messing around with the antenna, trying to improve the reception. As the familiar and reassuring voice of Walter Cronkite filled the room, Dad retreated to his recliner and leaned back, elevating the footrest.

"Shh, you girls stop your nonsense. Hurry up, Mother," he called out. "You're missing the broadcast."

"Never mind," Beth said to Cathy. "It'll probably turn up."

"Yes, yes, I'm coming," Mom called back down the stairs. "Can I bring anything for anyone? More pie?"

Her offer was greeted by a chorus of groans from the overstuffed family and a polite, "No, thank you," from Debbie.

Mom clattered down the stairs, still wearing her dress shoes and an apron over her dress, and took her place in her upright upholstered chair across from Dad.

"What did I miss?" she asked.

Dad put his fingers to his lips, motioning for her to be quiet. "Nothing yet, it just started."

The family sat in rapt attention, watching the black and white picture of the moon, as seen through a window in the

Apollo 8 spacecraft, and listening to the astronauts describe what they saw below on the surface of the moon—the craters and the potential landing site they called the Sea of Tranquility. Their voices were surprisingly clear, although occasionally drowned out by static. Beth marveled that they were getting this sound and picture from more than 238,000 miles away.

Soon, her mind wandered from the picture on the TV screen to wonder about Crystal. Had she been imagining things? Was she still alive, out there, somewhere? Beth didn't believe it but, if she was, would she go back to living with Allen in that sleazy whorehouse? The poor girl.

Beth looked around at her family. Her dad was nodding off in his recliner. Her brother, sister, and her mother were all intent on the TV screen, seeming to want to commit to memory this historic occasion. Debbie seemed distracted and gazed off in the distance. She had been sort of lost in her thoughts all evening. Gary glanced over at Debbie, smiled, squeezed her hand, and then turned back to the broadcast. *What was Debbie worrying about?* Beth wondered.

Beth tuned back in as the voice of one of the astronauts described the moon as "foreboding...stark...unappetizing." *He sounds homesick for Earth,* she thought. *I bet he wonders if he'll ever get home again.* She glanced around her, appreciating the cozy family scene. As the half-hour program neared its end, the three astronauts took turns reading from the book of Genesis in the Bible. Beth leaned over and tapped her father's foot to wake him. He wouldn't want to miss this.

Frank Borman concluded, "And God called the dry land Earth, and the gathering together of the waters called the Seas: and God saw that it was good. And from the crew of Apollo 8, we close with good night, good luck, a Merry Christmas—and God bless all of you, all of you on the good Earth."

The family all sighed and stirred as Dad righted himself in his recliner and got up to turn off the TV. "Well, that was really something," he said. "That made up for a lot. At least one good thing happened in 1968."

After the show, gifts were distributed and opened and a few more cookies were consumed. Then Gary drove Beth home.

As he pulled up in front of her house, Beth said, "Just a minute. Turn on the overhead light, will you? I want to show you something. But first, promise me you won't say anything about it to anyone else without talking to me first. Okay?"

"Okay," he said slowly as he reached up and switched on the dome light.

Beth dug through her purse and pulled out the small picture of Crystal and handed it to Gary. "Have you ever seen this girl?" she asked.

He crinkled his brow, and then his look of puzzlement turned to one of astonishment.

"Where did you get this picture? How do you know her?" he asked.

Beth gave him an abbreviated version of what had happened and then said, "So, I'm trying to find her—if she's still alive.

Or, find out who killed her, if she's not. But, don't spread it around. I don't want Mom and Dad to know. As far as they're concerned, I saw a girl who got drunk, fell down the hill, and then got up and walked away. That's Bill Crample's version of events."

"But you don't think he's right, do you?"

"No, I don't."

"Why don't you leave it to the police? It isn't safe for you to mess around in this."

"I would, but they don't seem to think anything serious happened. And, from Crample's reaction, I don't think he cares a whole lot, either way. He'd just as soon let it go because that makes his job easier."

"Yeah, you could be right about that. He's not exactly a go-getter."

"So, have you seen her?"

"Maybe." Gary hesitated, and Beth wondered if there was something he didn't want her to know. But, she didn't believe that. He and Debbie had been sweethearts since high school. He wouldn't mess around like that, would he?

"Well?" she prompted him.

"Promise me that you won't do anything crazy," he said. "If you get hurt, I'll kill you."

Beth laughed, and said, "I promise. Nobody wants me safe more than I do."

He looked at her skeptically, then stared at the photo. "Yeah, I might have seen her. I think I saw her at the Big Boy restaurant."

Beth felt a chill go down her spine. "Really? When was that?"

"One Saturday night, a few weeks back. I first noticed her standing outside by the door, like she was waiting for someone. We passed her when Debbie and I went in. I didn't recognize her, so I kind of looked closer to see who she was, and I noticed that her eyes were red, like she'd been crying. I didn't think too much of it at the time, but after we sat in a booth I could see her through the window, waiting, and then a big black car came up and she climbed in."

"Did you see who was driving?"

"No, but I recognized the car. It belongs to the banker, Mr. Brown, and I wondered what was going on." He handed the photo back to her and turned off the dome light.

"Very interesting. Thanks." Beth started to get out of the car.

"Wait," Gary said. "So now what? What are you going to do about it?"

"I don't know. Maybe nothing. Maybe I'll tell Crample." She yawned. "Right now, I'm just going to get ready for bed. Thanks for the ride."

Once inside, Beth carefully locked the door behind her and slid on the chain lock before she plopped her bag of gifts down on the coffee table. Chestnut came over and rubbed against her legs while she took off her wraps. She reached down to pet him.

"Such a good kitty," she said. He meowed in agreement. Beth made herself a cup of tea and then sat down to enjoy the interlude of peace and quiet. Tomorrow, they would all meet again and, after church, go to Grandma's house for another round of gift-giving and feasting.

Later, Chestnut sat on the bathmat and watched Beth as she brushed her teeth and reflected on the day. Everyone had seemed to like their gifts. Even her sister had exclaimed happily over the little charm Beth gave her and then ran to get her charm bracelet and add it on.

Soon, her mind drifted to the day after tomorrow, when she would resume the search for Crystal. One way or the other, alive or dead, she would find her. Beth wasn't sure why she felt so determined. Perhaps it was because she always felt surrounded by the love of her family, even when they were far away, and Crystal had no one else to look out for her.

Chapter 10

Beth inhaled the smell of library books and sighed, relieved to be back at work and away from the cacophony of noise and voices that had been the ambient background sound of the last two days of back-to-back Christmas festivities. It had been fun to see Grandma and all the other relatives, but it was also stimulation overload.

Peace at last, she thought. At least she had gotten a chance to ask her brother about her car. He'd assured her it would be done before the beginning of winter quarter.

Pounding and drilling startled her, interrupting her train of thought.

Oh, right, she recalled. *Workmen would be here for the next few days building a vestibule inside the front door.* Maybe she could find a quieter place to work. She hurried through the stacks to the librarian's office and knocked on the door.

"Come in," Miss Tanner called out.

Beth cracked opened the door and leaned in. Miss Tanner was sitting behind her desk, books and papers spread out in front of her, looking frazzled. Her red, bouffant hairdo leaned to one side and pencils were sticking out of it above each ear.

"Miss Tanner, is it okay if I start by shelf reading the reference section in the basement?" Beth asked.

"Yes, that would be fine. I realize the noise is quite deafening. Hopefully, they'll be done with the worst of it in a few days. I also hope the disruption is worth it, in the long run. Now, run along, and close the door behind you."

Beth left, scampered down the steps, and flipped on the lights in the reference room. *Much better*, she thought as the sound receded behind her to a bearable level. She grabbed a cart for any misshelved books she might find and rolled it over to the beginning of the Dewey decimal system, which started with general encyclopedias. She ran a finger along the call numbers, looking for any that were out of place. A few volumes had been put back in the wrong order. She reordered them; an easy fix.

She'd gotten into the 133 numbers when her finger paused on the spine of *An Encyclopedia of Occultism*. Hmmm, maybe it had information about the ring that she and Evie had found in the snow. It might be an occult item. She pulled the book off the shelf. It had pictures on the front cover, so maybe it was illustrated. There might even be a picture of the ring. But, what would she look for? She had no idea what it was called, so how could she find it?

She took the book to a nearby wooden table, its surface etched with initials by generations of young library patrons, pulled out a heavy wooden chair, sat down, and opened it.

Glancing through the first few pages, she was disappointed to see that there were very few illustrations. She was about to give up and place it back on the shelf, when Miss Tanner walked into the room, followed by Mr. Flack, the editor of the local newspaper. His bald head reflected the light and his small eyes peaked out from folds of fat.

Beth hastily closed the book and stood up. The librarian looked from Beth to the book, and then to the spot on the shelf where the book had been.

"I was just…" Beth trailed off.

"Oh yes, well, one must keep learning. Curiosity is an excellent trait in a library employee," Miss Tanner said. Her voice was pitched higher than normal and her smile looked forced. "Beth, Mr. Flack is here to do some research. He'll be in the back, looking at microfilm."

Turning to him, she said, "Mr. Flack, you remember Miss Williams, don't you? If you need any assistance, Beth will be happy to help you."

"Oh, yes, of course. Beth, is it?" he mumbled. Clearly not remembering her at all. With that, he turned and waddled off in the direction of the microfilm cabinets and reader.

Miss Tanner drummed her polished red nails on the tabletop, and let her forced smile fall. "You'd think we could have a few days without dealing with library patrons. But, what could I say? After all, he is an important library supporter. He shouldn't take up too much of your time. I think he knows where everything is and how to use the microfilm reader."

Beth was relieved that Miss Tanner's ire was directed toward Mr. Flack, and not caused by her goofing off while she was supposed to be working.

Miss Tanner turned her attention to the book lying on the table. "I didn't realize you had an interest in the occult," she said.

"Well, I don't. Not really. I was looking for something. But I don't think I'll find it. I don't know what it's called, you see, so I can't very well look it up."

Miss Tanner's eyes brightened with interest. "Tell me more. What is this thing that you're looking for?"

"Well, I found a very unusual ring. It was silver and had a carved stone on it. The picture carved into the stone was bizarre. It was a sort of person, but with a rooster's head, his legs were made of snakes, and he was holding a whip."

"Oh, my. You say you found this ring? Where did you find it?"

"Near where I saw that girl fall down the hill last week. Remember? We went back the next day to look around."

"Yes, I remember. It's not the sort of thing one readily forgets. We? You said, 'we went back.' Was there someone else with you when you found this ring?"

"Yes. Actually, Evie Hanson found it. She was with me."

"Indeed. Can I see it? Do you have it with you?"

"No, I don't have it with me," Beth said. She didn't want to explain that she had already lost or misplaced it.

"Well, I can't be sure without seeing it, but it sounds like what you're describing is called an abraxas stone. Let's see…" She flipped through the pages of the book. "Oh, yes, here's the entry." She squinted, and then put on the reading glasses that were hanging on a chain around her neck. "'The Basilidian sect of Gnostics, of the second century, claimed Abraxas as their supreme god.' Okay, yes, and…" she read on silently for a few moments while running her finger down the entry. "Ah, here's the description near the end, 'He is represented on ancient amulets, with a whip in his hand…' Yes, yes…" She made a clicking sound with her tongue as she continued to skim the article, and then resumed reading out loud. "'Many stones and gems cut in various symbolic forms, such as the head of a fowl, a serpent, and so forth, were worn by the Basilidians as amulets.' That sounds like what you described. Doesn't it?"

"Yes, I think so," Beth said. "But, what would someone around here be doing with something like that? I doubt that we have any of those—what did you call them, Basilidians?—around here."

"No, probably not. It is odd. Here. Why don't you read all about it?" Miss Tanner handed Beth the reference book. "And, I'd like to have a look at that ring. If you'd care to bring it in."

"The thing is—I don't have it, right now. I think Evie might have it." Beth felt the heat rising in her cheeks. She was sure Miss Tanner could tell she was lying.

"I see." Miss Tanner scrutinized Beth. "Well, suit yourself. At any rate, after you read that entry, you'd better get back to work. You have a lot of ground to cover before the library reopens." Miss Tanner turned and strode out of the room and up the stairs.

The whirring sound of microfilm being rewound announced that Mr. Flack had finished with one reel.

Beth poked her head into the room.

"Just put that in the basket," she said, pointing to a wire basket on top of the microfilm cabinets. "I'll put it away, later."

"Are you sure? I'd be happy to put it back where I got it," Mr. Flack said.

"No. We prefer to do it ourselves, so we know what's being used. Are you finding what you're looking for?"

"Yes, thank you. Of course, some things will have to wait until I can get to the cities and go to the U of M library. The resources here are very good for a small public library. But, one can only expect so much. Even the Ag school library, and the State College of North Dakota's library in Grand Bend don't have everything I need."

"Is that so? What are you working on?" Beth immediately regretted raising the question. Mr. Flack was known to be long-winded at times.

"I'm researching the New Age phenomenon, and planning to write a book on it. Interest in the subject is high, with the so-called 'dawning of the Age of Aquarius.' I happened to overhear you talking to Miss Tanner about the occult. Is that something you have a particular interest in?"

"Well, it is interesting," Beth said. "But, I wouldn't say a particular interest. No."

Over the next fifteen minutes, Mr. Flack proceeded to lay out the rough outline of his book. He was getting into chapter-by-chapter descriptions while Beth shifted from one foot to another. Finally, he seemed to notice her lack of attention and wound up his soliloquy.

"As I was saying, even in a small town, such as Davison City, one finds elements of New Age practices. That is how I came to be interested in learning more about it."

This captured Beth's attention. "New Age practices in Davison City? Such as Gnostic practices?"

"Why yes." Mr. Flack seemed delighted by the question. "It is an open secret that certain members of our community are investigating Gnosticism."

"Beth, oh Beth, are you there?" Miss Tanner called down the stairs.

"Excuse me, Mr. Flack," Beth said, and then she hurried out to the bottom of the stairs.

"Yes, I'm here, Miss Tanner."

"Phone call for you, dear. I believe it's your father."

"Okay, I'll be right up," Beth said.

She hurried back to the microfilm room. "I have to take a phone call, Mr. Flack. But, I'd be interested in continuing our conversation. Will you be here for a while?"

"Sorry, I have to get back to the office. I'd be delighted to speak to you again, when you get a chance."

"Okay, and if you need me to pick up a book for you from the North Dakota State College library, let me know. I'm a student there."

"Thank you. That is very kind. I may take you up on that offer," he said.

Later, Evie and Beth sat in a booth at the Big Boy restaurant. The reference book, which Miss Tanner had reluctantly let Beth take out of the library overnight after she promised to bring it back the very next day, sat on the table between them.

After Evie read the article, she said, "Wow. So, what do you think? Was it a Basilidian Gnostic, a demon worshiper, or a follower of the Egyptian gods who dropped that ring?"

Beth laughed, then said, "Pretty wild, isn't it? It could be, though. Maybe it belongs to one of our local New Agers." She told Evie what Mr. Flack had said.

"I can't believe it. Practicing Gnostics, right here in Davison City? Who are they?" Evie asked.

"I don't know. Our conversation was interrupted by a phone call from my dad. He wanted to know if I needed a ride home," Beth said.

"Did you?"

"Not really, but since he was going to be passing right by, I took advantage of getting a warm car ride home. But seriously, about that ring, it's probably just a cheap imitation that some hippy-dippy type guy bought because he thought it looked cool," Beth said.

"I don't know, it seemed real enough to me. It had a heft to it, so it's not made of plastic, tin, or anything. Have you found it yet?" Evie said.

"No. I asked my sister about it, but she denied ever seeing it. You don't think anyone came in and stole it, do you? My door was open when I got home that night."

"Unlikely. It probably was mislaid. How hard have you looked?"

"Well, not too hard. Between the holiday stuff and going back to work, I haven't had time to do much at home except eat, sleep, and take care of Chestnut." She paused and scrunched up her face. "I feel kind of guilty about being gone so much. I think Chestnut misses me. When I'm home, he follows me around, and sleeps on me every chance he gets."

"Ah, that's sweet. And, I'm sure he's happy to see you; but cats are fine being on their own a lot of the time, too."

"If you say so. You're the expert. Having a pet is a new thing for me."

"Do you want me to help you look for the ring? We should still turn it in to the police if we can find it, don't you think?"

"I guess so. How about Saturday. Can you come over then?"

"Sure."

The waitress came over to take their orders. Evie said, "Hi, Sally. How's it going?"

She looked familiar to Beth, but she couldn't quite place her. After she wrote down their orders and left, Beth asked Evie, "Do you know her?"

"Kind of. She was a couple of years ahead of us in school—in my older brother's class."

"Should we ask her about Crystal?"

"We could. There's probably no point beating around the bush. I bet that everyone in town has heard about how you found the dead girl by now."

"Right, but remember. The story we're sticking to is that she isn't dead, just missing."

"Got it," Evie said. "So, you said that your brother Gary saw her here. Right?"

"Yeah, she was standing outside the door and then Gary saw the banker's car pull up, and she got in."

"Was that the night she disappeared?"

"No, a different Saturday night."

Sally headed back toward their table with their beverages. Beth dug the small photo of Crystal out of her purse and held it out toward Evie.

"Since you know her, why don't you ask her about it?"

"No problem." Evie took the photo. "Hey, Sally, got a minute?"

"Sure. What's up?"

"Have you heard about the girl that Beth saw fall down the hill in the park last weekend?"

Sally glanced at Beth. "Yeah, but I heard she was dead."

"Just stunned, I guess," Beth said. "Apparently, she got up and wandered off. She's gone missing, so maybe she has amnesia or something."

"No kidding?"

"Yeah. So anyway, here's her picture," Evie said. "Have you ever seen this girl?"

Sally wiped her hands on her apron and gingerly held the small picture by its edges while examining it. "Yeah, I think so. But, she looks kinda different now. Older. But I think it's the same girl."

"When did you see her?" Evie asked.

"I saw her more than once. Mostly on Saturday nights, I think. She'd hang around outside, ya know. I guess she was waiting for a ride or something. Then, after a while, she'd be gone. She never came in—it was weird. We all kinda talk about it. I mean, if she thought nobody noticed, she was way off."

"Did you ever see who picked her up?" Evie asked.

"Saturday is always a busy night, so I didn't watch her or nothing, but one time I saw her getting into a car."

"Did you see who was driving the car, or did you recognize the car?"

"Well, I didn't see who was driving, so I'm not sure, but I think it was that lawyer's car."

"What lawyer is that?"

"You know, Mr. Nobis. He has that Ford Mustang, even though he's much too old to be driving it, in my opinion. He has a hard time getting out of it."

They all laughed.

"Was she here last Saturday night?" Evie asked.

"I don't know. I didn't work that shift. But, I could ask around if you want."

"Sure, okay. If it's not too much trouble. Give me a call if you find out anything."

"No problem. But, why do you guys care? I mean, is she a friend of yours or something?"

Evie looked at Beth, and they both shrugged.

Beth said, "No, we don't know her. I guess, since I was the last one to see her, I want to find out what happened to her, and it's kind of a mystery. I mean, where did she go?"

Chapter 11

"Do you realize it has already been one week since you found the body in the park?" Evie asked, her voice muffled as she knelt, head down, wedged between the couch and the coffee table, shining a flashlight back and forth across the dust balls under Beth's couch. Chestnut sat atop a pile of magazines on the coffee table, watching her, his tail twitching from side to side.

Kerchoo. Evie sneezed and sat up on her heels. This sent Chestnut rocketing off the coffee table, scattering magazines behind him. He took shelter under the bookshelves.

"Hey, Beth, how long has it been since you vacuumed under this thing?"

"What?" Beth poked her head around the corner of the kitchen door.

"I said, how long has it been since you vacuumed under this thing."

"Vacuum—what's that? I don't know. How long have I lived here—three, maybe four months?

"Oh my God!" Evie said as she grasped her chest in mock horror. "You do realize that your mother doesn't live here, don't you?" She got up and dusted off the knees of her jeans. "Find anything in the kitchen?"

Beth walked over and plopped down in the chair. "Nope. I examined every crack and crevice. I even took the little plastic doohickey off the bottom of the fridge. Nada. If the ring rolled off the table, as you said, it must have rolled out of the room."

"Or, maybe it was knocked out," Evie said, pointing to Chestnut. He stared back at her as though he realized he was being accused of something.

"Oh...right," Beth turned and eyed him with suspicion. "If that's the case, it could be anywhere in the apartment." She sighed. "How about taking a break, and then I'll dig out the vacuum before we resume the search."

"Sounds good to me, but you don't have to clean on my account," Evie said.

"Too late. You already made me feel guilty about my abysmal housekeeping. Come on, let's have some tea." Beth headed to the kitchen and Evie followed.

Once they were seated at the kitchen table, cradling cups of tea, Evie said, again, "Like I was saying, it's been a week since you saw the body roll down the hill in the park, and then it disappeared. So, what have we learned?"

"Well, according to her pimp, Crystal was last seen alive when he dropped her off in the Big Boy parking lot last Saturday."

"Not what you'd call an unimpeachable witness."

"For sure. By the way, did the Big Boy waitress, Sally, ever get back to you saying if anyone else saw Crystal there last Saturday?"

"Not yet."

"Right, so, what else?"

"Well, you found out that the ring is some kind of occult thing. Of course, it could just be fake and not related to the case. But, it would be nice to have someone take a closer look at it."

"We could show it to Mr. Gloor, the jeweler. He would know if it's real, I suppose." Beth stared into her cup as she spooned in another heaping teaspoon of sugar and stirred it in. "And, we could show it to Miss Tanner. She asked to see it when she caught me looking it up at work. I told her you had it."

"Me? Why did you tell her that?"

"I don't know. I suppose I felt dumb claiming to have found this ring, but not being able to produce it. I didn't want to admit that I'd mislaid or lost it. She already seems to think I'm scatterbrained. Sorry about that."

"No big deal. We both found it, so I guess I could have kept it instead of you."

Beth sipped her tea, and stared out the window for a few minutes, then said, "I suppose there's no harm in her knowing about the ring, or thinking that you have it. After all, we know she's not involved. For one thing, why would she be? Anyway, she was in the library when I got there after I saw the body, so she's definitely in the clear. When we find the ring, we should show it to her. She knows about a lot of different stuff, including most of what goes on in this town."

"If we find it," Evie added.

"True. Also, maybe we should stake out the Big Boy tonight."

"Are you serious?"

"Why not? It's Saturday night. Whoever picked up Crystal last Saturday might come back there tonight for another one of Al's girls."

"Isn't that dangerous? What if we're seen?"

"It's pitch dark by 6:00 at night. We can park at the edge of the lot, where we have a good view of the place, turn off our lights, and nobody will notice us. Besides, chances are nothing will happen. We'll just sit there for a while and then go inside for a hamburger. What puzzles me is the discrepancy between what my brother said, that he saw the banker, Mr. Brown, pick Crystal up, and what Sally said, that it was the lawyer, Mr. Nobis."

"They both could be right. It could have been those two, and other men, too. After all, she was a prostitute. If Sally is working tonight, we can ask her for an update on what other people who work there have seen."

"Yeah, I suppose. So, what do you say? Do you want to go on a stakeout?"

"Well, I do like the Big Boy hamburgers. Count me in." Evie grinned. "Once we finish our tea, I'll call my mom and let her know I won't be home for dinner, while you dig out that vacuum cleaner."

"I hate to say it, but it sounds like the game is afoot," Beth said.

Evie groaned, rolled her eyes, and they both laughed.

A couple of hours later, they'd finished shifting furniture and cleaning under it, sorting and stacking piles of magazines, and discarding newspapers. But, they hadn't found the ring.

Beth switched off the vacuum. "I give up. It's just not here. I don't understand it. Maybe my sister took it after all, and she wanted to keep it so she lied about taking it. That isn't like her, but what else could have happened?"

"I don't know," Evie said.

They slouched down on the couch and stared, blankly, into space. Chestnut, who had been hiding under the bookshelves sheltering from the vacuum cleaner, laid on his back, reached his front paws over his head, and swatted at something behind one of the cement blocks that held up the bottom shelf. It made a clanking sound.

Beth sat bolt upright. "What was that?" She dashed over, knelt, and reached forward. She felt a hard, round object, and pulled it out. "Look," she held it up. "It's the ring. Good kitty, you helped us find it."

Beth and Evie danced around in excitement, while Chestnut hunkered down, and glowered at them for stealing his toy.

That evening, Beth and Evie sat in Evie's car under the shadow of scraggly pine trees planted as a windbreak around the perimeter of the Big Boy parking lot. As soon as Evie had turned off the car, the temperature inside the car started to drop. Now, Beth clenched her teeth together to keep them from chattering, buried her icy nose in her neck scarf, and hugged her coat closer.

Evie glanced over at Beth. "Do you think we should start the car so we can get some heat in here?"

"Not yet. Give it a few more minutes," Beth said. "We should know soon if something is going to happen."

"Okay, five more minutes, then I'm taking a chance on breaking our cover rather than turn into a Popsicle." Evie stomped her feet on the floorboards, trying to warm them.

"Shh, stay quiet," Beth said.

"Nobody will hear me. Nobody is out there," Evie said. She crossed her arms across her chest and banged her mittens against her arms. "I suppose we should drop the ring off with the police, once we've shown it to the jeweler and Miss Tanner."

"I suppose, for all the good it will do. Crample will probably just dump it in lost and found. After all, as far as he's concerned, there is no crime. Just a girl who decided to take off for parts unknown."

"Yeah, maybe. But wasn't he going to look up the license plate number from the photo? You could ask him about that, too."

"What if he won't tell me, or if he never did look it up?"

"Oh, I think he'll tell you if you ask him nicely," Evie said.

"What's that supposed to mean."

"You know what I mean. He's into you."

"No he's not," Beth laughed. "You're nuts."

"Am I? Why do you think he asked you to go out to Al's with him? He wanted a chance to get to know you."

"I doubt it. He hardly spoke to me the whole way there and back."

"Well, I think he's into you, but he's shy. His whole family is shy. They hardly ever come out of the house except when they have to, and none of his brothers or sisters are married, and they're all grown up. The family is kinda odd. Ask your dad. I think he's done some handyman work on their place."

"Huh, maybe you're right—about the odd part, I mean— not the "he likes you" part. My dad did say something about how he could tell me a thing or two about the Cramples."

"I told you—" Evie started to say when Beth cut her off.

"Look," Beth pointed at a car on the highway as it slowed, and then turned into the restaurant's driveway. When it passed under one of the lights lining the outer edge of the parking lot, they could see that it was a purple Cadillac. "Look at that.

Could that be Al's pimp-mobile?" She laughed. "Not exactly subtle, is it?"

The car stopped near the restaurant door, and a girl got out of the passenger side. She was wearing a puffy winter coat, a short skirt, and knee-high boots. Her head was uncovered, and her hair was arranged into an updo. She walked over to the side of the building as the purple car pulled away. She didn't approach the door; instead, she huddled by the side of the building, rooted through her purse, pulled out a pack of cigarettes and a lighter, and lit one.

"Good Lord! I hope she doesn't have to wait long to be picked up," Evie said. "Do you recognize her? Is she one of Al's girls?"

"I'm not sure. She could be. To tell the truth, I didn't pay too much attention to them. And, when I saw them, they weren't all dolled up."

A few minutes passed, and then a dark-colored car approached.

"That's not a Mustang—so, not the lawyer's car," Beth said. "Unless he's driving a different car today."

The car drove up to the restaurant, stopped, the girl got in, and then it drove off.

"There they go," Beth said. "Let's follow them. But, don't get too close. I don't want them to see us."

Evie started her car and followed the other car out of the driveway as it turned right and headed toward town. Soon, the car they were following sped up, as though they'd noticed they were being followed.

"Don't let him get away," Beth said. "At least get close enough so we can get a good look at the car and get the license plate number."

Beth dug through her purse and came up with a notebook and pen. She leaned forward, trying to see past the fog forming on the cold windshield as the heater blasted warm air onto it. She wiped a portal with the edge of her sleeve.

"I think it's black, maybe a Pontiac." She rubbed at the windshield again. "The license plate starts with 7, I think. Can you speed up any more?"

"I'll try, but this old beater isn't built for speed," Evie said as she floored the accelerator. The car lurched forward, and slowly picked up speed.

When the car they were following got to the outskirts of town, it turned right at the first crossroads. Evie followed, turning sharply right, her tires squealing.

"I don't see them," she said. They must have turned again. Which way should I go?"

"Try left," Beth said.

Evie turned left. Two blocks ahead, they saw the car speed through an orange light. They drove up to the light, which now was red, and stopped.

"Damn it, damn it! We've lost them," Evie said. "Sorry about that."

"It's not your fault. You tried," Beth said. She was a bit relieved. She realized that they didn't have a plan about what to do if they caught up with the car, outside of identifying the driver, or seeing where they stopped. And, if they got close enough to identify the driver, then he could also identify them, which she didn't want.

"Did you get any more of the license plate number?" Evie asked.

"I think it was HF-something, but that's as far as I got. My brother might know who has a black Pontiac with a license plate number beginning with 7HF. He has an amazing memory when it comes to cars. I'll ask him." As they waited for the light to turn green, she asked, "Well, what now? Back to the Big Boy?"

"Sounds good to me. I haven't had that hamburger, yet," Evie said. She drove around the block, and they headed back in that direction.

Seated back at the restaurant, they learned that Sally wasn't working. She had been out sick for a couple of days. After they ordered, Beth went to the phone booth and called her brother. A few minutes later, she returned. "You'll never guess what Gary said about the car we followed."

"What?"

"It belongs to the jeweler."

"You're kidding."

"No, I'm not. Gary said he was sure. He just worked on that car last week."

"Oh my God, Mr. Gloor is picking up prostitutes? He's a married man."

They stopped talking while the waitress delivered the baskets of hamburgers and fries and tall glasses of soda.

"Apparently, not happily married," Beth said after the waitress left.

"That's crazy. So, three separate men, that we know of, have picked up one of Al's girls here. I wonder how many of the men in this town are in on this. Do you think this is related to Crystal's death, or is this just a handy pickup point?"

"I don't know. But one thing is certain. We can't show the ring to Mr. Gloor. He could be a suspect."

"Agreed," Evie said, and then took a big bite out of her burger.

Chapter 12

Sunday, December 29, 1968.

Beth took a short detour to the railroad station to check on Saturday's arrivals and departures. She scrutinized the schedule posted on the wall. It had suddenly occurred to her, while walking to church, to wonder why Crystal was at the railroad station on the night she died. Had she been there to catch a train, or meet someone who was arriving? There it was—an eastbound to Chicago was scheduled to stop at 5:00 p.m.

How stupid of me not to have thought of this sooner, Beth thought. She walked up to the ticket window.

"Hello, is anyone there," she called out.

A few moments passed, and then an elderly man wearing a railway uniform shambled up to the window. "Yes, can I help you?" he asked.

"I'm wondering about the Saturday train to Chicago." She dug through the contents of her purse.

"Do you want a ticket?" he asked.

"No, that's not it." She retrieved the small picture of Crystal and handed it across to him. "I'm wondering if you sold a ticket to this girl a week ago, Saturday the 21st."

"I don't know. Let me take a closer look." He squinted at the picture while moving it back and forth, as though to get it into focus, and then slid it back across the counter to Beth. "Maybe, can't say for sure. There was a girl here that night. Might have been her."

"Was she here waiting for someone? Or, did she buy a ticket for Chicago?"

"Not waiting. No. I don't think so. I don't recall anyone waiting here. There was a girl—could have been this one—who bought a ticket for the twin cities."

"Do you know if she got on the train?"

"Nope. Once I sell the tickets, I don't pay no more attention. Why do you want to know?" He fixed her with a suspicious stare.

"Just wondering, that's all. Well, thanks," Beth mumbled.

"Anything else? Do you want to buy a ticket?"

"No," she started to turn away, then turned back. "Is there a schedule I can take with me?"

"Over there." He gestured toward a display rack and shuffled off.

Beth took one from the rack. If someone was expecting Crystal at the other end, maybe there might be a way to find out who that person was, and then find out more about Crystal. That seemed unlikely, though. A lot of people must have been at the station in Minneapolis that night. Even if there was such a person, how would she figure out who had been there to meet Crystal? It seemed like a slim hope. Still, she dropped the schedule into her purse and then carefully stowed the picture into an inside, zippered compartment, along with the ring. "No more misplacing items," she scolded herself.

After Sunday mass, as they'd arranged, Beth waited for Evie in the vestibule of the church.

"Ready to go?" she asked.

"Sure, just a sec. I'll say goodbye to Mom." Evie talked to her mom, who turned and gave Beth a weak smile. When she came back, she said, "Mom wasn't too thrilled with me scampering off before the obligatory Sunday after church family meal, but she'll get over it. So, what's up? You said you had some ideas about what to do next."

"Right. I'll tell you all about it while you warm up the car."

They hurried out of the church and down the block. Soon, they were seated in Evie's car. Beth told Evie about stopping at the railroad station.

"I don't know if that helps at all. One thought I had was that I could take the train to Minneapolis next Saturday night, and see if anyone hangs around the station after everyone else leaves. And then I could talk to them, and show them her picture. What do you think?"

"That seems like a long shot," Evie said.

"Yeah, I guess I'm clutching at straws." Beth sighed, loudly. "It's only a week until winter quarter starts and then, between school and my job at the library, we won't have much time to investigate. I was hoping we could make some progress on this case before then."

Beth lapsed into silence as she watched the last few parishioners trickle out of the church while the engine hummed. Her parents and sister were among the last to leave. Her dad had probably stopped, as usual, to swap tall tales with Father McClure.

"Me too," Evie said, and then paused to think. "How about this? We could go out to…to…you know, where Crystal was staying."

"You mean, the whorehouse?"

"Yeah, but that sounds so horrible. Let's call it Al's place. Anyway, we could go there and talk to the girl he dropped off at the Big Boy last night."

Beth grinned. "Not bad. Why didn't I think of that?"

"Thanks, I think. You can't have all the good ideas."

Beth said. "That girl, or the other one, might know where Crystal went the day she died. Maybe it was a regular appointment."

"Could be. She was seen being picked up by different men, but always on a Saturday night. But what about Al? He probably won't let us talk to them," Evie said.

"True. But, he can't always be home. Maybe he's out looking for a new girl to replace Crystal, or drumming up business. Let's go out there and see if his car is there."

Evie put the car in gear.

Beth said, "Go north and then take the highway heading toward Grand Bend. I'll tell you where to turn after that."

As they approached the bend in the road outside of town, where it turned west, Beth noticed a pickup truck pull up and stop on the side of the road. A couple of college-aged guys, probably from the local agriculture college, got out and began to haul a battered sofa out of the truck bed. There was a drop-off, down to a low spot next to the river, which was used as an unofficial dump.

"Litterbugs," Beth said. "I suppose they are clearing out their dorm room."

"That reminds me," Evie said. "I have to go to Grand Bend tomorrow and see about changing my schedule for next quarter. Somehow, I managed to sign up for two classes that are at the same time. So, I have to drop one of them and see what else is still available. I'll probably stand in line for hours, and end up with a class I hate, just to fill out my schedule, so I can keep my financial aid. Do you want to come with me for moral support?"

"Sounds fun." Beth groaned and rolled her eyes. "Wish I could, but I have to go to work tomorrow. While I'm there, I can show the ring to Miss Tanner, and let you know what she says."

"Then are you going to turn it over to the police?"

"I suppose so, for all the good it'll do. Since Crample doesn't believe there's a crime, he definitely won't see it as a clue."

"True. Still, someone may have reported losing it. If you talk to him and flirt a little, maybe he'll tell you all about it."

"Ha, ha," Beth said sarcastically, then stopped and thought for a moment. "I suppose it's worth a try. I'll have to practice batting my eyes in the mirror first."

She demonstrated for Evie, batting her eyes and pursing her lips. Evie started to giggle at the exaggeration, and swerved to the right, then sharply turned left again to stay on the road.

"Watch out!" Beth yelled.

"Your fault. You made me laugh," Evie said, stifling a laugh. Then, in a more serious tone, she said, "Just tell me when to turn."

"It's not far, past the windbreak and the silos. I'll let you know."

Beth turned on the radio and they sang along with the chorus of "Hey Jude," and other hits, as they rolled along.

Evie slowed the car as they drew close to Al's place, but they couldn't see the house. Evergreen bushes and trees obscured it.

Beth switched off the radio. "Turn into the driveway, but slowly," she whispered.

"Why are you whispering," Evie whispered back. "He can't hear us from here."

She turned into the driveway and inched toward the house. Al's flashy purple car, parked in front of the house, was the first thing they saw.

"Abort, abort," Beth said. "Back up."

Evie reversed out of the driveway, turned back toward the highway, and then pulled off to the side of the road. "Now what?" she asked.

"Is there someplace we can hide and watch the house?" Beth asked.

They looked up and down across the flat, white landscape. In the distance, here and there, clumps of trees surrounded homesteads. The only thing moving was a lone snow hare. White against white, he hopped along on his big rear feet. Only the black tips along the top edges of his ears gave him away.

"Nope, not here," Beth said. "Maybe if we drive back toward the highway we'll find a spot. If Al heads toward Davison City or Grand Bend, he'll have to go that way."

"Good idea," Evie said.

As they drove along, on the left they passed what looked like a deserted farmstead, surrounded by a scraggly line of trees—a mixture of bare-branched deciduous trees and a few evergreens.

"How about here?" Evie slowed down as they approached. "No good. The driveway is completely drifted in." Evie continued driving, and soon they approached a farmstead on the right. "How about here? Do we dare? It looks like somebody lives here."

"Hmm," Beth considered as their car idled near the driveway. "Judging by the single set of tire tracks, it looks like someone's gone out and hasn't come back, yet. Okay, turn in, and we'll see if anyone comes out of the house."

As they slowly approached, Beth watched the house. No one came out, and the curtains didn't twitch.

"Looks like no one's home. Turn around, and drive back toward the road. Stop where we can watch for Al's car, as well as the owners coming home."

"What if they catch us in their driveway?" Evie asked.

"Chances are they won't. But even if they turn in before we have a chance to leave, the worst that can happen is that they'll ask us what we're doing here, and we'll say we got lost and pulled in to turn around. That's almost true."

They sat and let the car idle with the windows cracked and the radio turned down, and then waited.

"I can't stay too long," Evie said after a half hour had passed. "Jim might call at 4:00."

"Okay," Beth glanced at her watch. "It's only one. So you have plenty of time. How is Jim?"

"Fine."

Something in Evie's voice caused Beth to turn and look at her more closely. "What is it?"

"It's nothing, really. Just that our conversations are kind of stilted. I have to plan things in advance to talk about. He doesn't seem to make an effort. Of course, he never was much of a conversationalist—more a man of action. And, the longer we're apart, the less there is to say, it seems. We just repeat that we miss each other. Our calls keep getting shorter."

"That's probably perfectly normal. At least you can tell him about our investigation."

"Are you kidding? I can't tell him about that. He'd worry."

"Yeah, I suppose you're right. Well, tell him about school, Christmas, and…" Beth trailed off, unable to think of other safe topics. "Anyway, don't worry. Once he's home, everything will get back to normal."

"Yeah, I'm sure it will," Evie said. But, she didn't sound sure.

They fell back into their thoughts. Soon a roar and a purple blur announced Al's car passing by.

"Let's go," Beth said.

Chapter 13

Beth stood on the doorstep of Al's place with Evie behind her, peeking over her shoulder.

"Nobody is answering," Evie said. "Maybe we should go."

"Give it a minute. Maybe they have to put on some clothes."

The door cracked open.

"What?" a woman asked.

"Hi. Remember me? My name is Beth. I was here the other day. This is my friend, Evie."

"Oh yeah, I remember you. You came with that cop." The door opened a few more inches. A wan face, eyebrows plucked to a thin line, and topped by blond hair in rollers looked out. "What do you want?"

"We were wondering if we could ask you a few questions," Beth said.

"What about?" The door didn't open any further.

"About Crystal. Can we come in? It's freezing out here."

The girl turned away and said, "What do ya think, Dawn. Should I let them in?"

Beth couldn't make out the mumbled reply, but the door opened. The girl, who was wearing a pink terrycloth bathrobe, stepped aside and gestured them in.

"Okay, but just for a minute. You gotta be out of here before Al gets back. He don't like us talking to nobody 'cept him and the customers."

"Sure, no problem," Beth said.

A woman, her red hair also in rollers and wearing a bathrobe—hers was lilac—stood at the stove frying eggs. She must be the girl they saw at the Big Boy last night.

The smell made Beth's mouth water and reminded her that it was way past lunchtime. "Smell's good—Dawn, right?"

Dawn looked over her shoulder, a cigarette dangled from the corner of her mouth—that explained the mumbling.

"Yup, that's me," she said. "I'd offer you some," she gestured with the spatula, "but I only made enough for me and Sarah." She carefully etched around the edges of the eggs she was frying with the spatula, and then turned them gently.

"That's okay," Beth said, warily eying the crusted dishes sitting in the sink. She wondered if Dawn had washed her hands since the last time she'd done whatever it was she did. "Anyway, as I said, I'm Beth and this is my friend, Evie." She gestured toward Evie, standing next to her on the rug, her bangs sticking up from static electricity after removing her wool hat, and now unwrapping her scarf.

"Hi," Evie said. She smiled and raised a hand in greeting to both of them.

"Okay, now we're all acquainted," Sarah said. "What do you want to know?"

"We are trying to find Crystal," Beth said. "Have you seen her since the last time I was out here?"

Sarah and Dawn looked at each other and shrugged.

"Nope," Sarah said. "Don't care if I ever do, either."

"Really, why is that?" Evie asked.

Beth was busy removing her hat, gloves, and scarf. She was getting hot. *Boy, they sure liked to keep it warm in here.*

"She was kind of stuck up. Acted like she was better than us, or something. Always running off, and then Al would take her back when she crawled back." She snorted.

"So this happened how many times?" Evie asked.

"I don't know. A couple of times, I guess," Sarah said.

Dawn shuffled over in her slippers, a plate in each hand, and dropped the plates on the table, one in front of Sarah. She went back for a plate of toast and a mug of coffee, and sat down at the table.

"Oh, she wasn't so bad," Dawn said. "Al spoiled her, that's all. He had a soft spot for her. He shoulda knocked some sense into her."

"You don't say," Beth chimed in, now untangled from her scarf. "How long have you been living here?"

"About six or seven months. Wouldn't you say?" Dawn asked Sarah.

"Sounds about right," Sarah said.

"Do you know where Crystal came from, or have the names of any of her friends or family?"

They both shook their heads, no.

"How about her, ah, customers, do you know any of those?" Evie asked.

"Nope. I guess we're just not the confiding types," Sarah said, causing Dawn to giggle. "We got our own problems, ya know."

"Say, what's your interest, anyway? All of a sudden, everyone wants to know about Crystal. Crystal this, Crystal that," Dawn said.

"Who do you mean? Who else has been asking about her?" Beth said.

Dawn stiffened, her lips forming a thin line. "Just you and those, those freaks…" she trailed off.

"Freaks? What freaks?"

"Never mind. Mind your own business. Anyway, you better get outa here. Al will be back soon. He just went to get a carton of smokes." Dawn stubbed out her cigarette in an overflowing ashtray, picked up a fork, and impaled the yolk of one of her eggs, releasing a golden stream.

"Okay, we'll go. But, do you mind if we take another peek at her room, first?" Beth asked.

"Won't do you no good," Sarah said as she wiped up the yolk with a triangle of toast. "Her stuff is all gone."

"Gone? Gone where?" Beth asked.

"Al said we should take what we wanted, bundle up the rest of her junk, and put it out by the trash burner. He needs that bedroom for a new girl he's gonna bring in. Guess he decided Crystal is gone for good this time."

"Okay, well thanks for your time," Beth said, and then they left.

"Wait a sec," Evie said, as they headed out to her car.

"What?"

"Let's look at what's out by the trash burner, and see if her stuff is still there."

"Good idea," Beth said.

They headed along an uneven path trampled into the snow, around the back of the house. They found the trash burner surrounded by a small pile of trash bags.

"Looks like they haven't been keeping up with burning their trash. We might be in luck," Beth said.

They pulled open several bags full of frozen kitchen waste, empty cans, bottles, and other assorted junk. Finally, Beth opened one that was full of mostly paper, old movie posters with scotch tape along the edges, old cracked records, and more.

"Evie, look at this," she said.

"Jackpot!" Evie said. "Do you think Al would know if we just took it?"

"I doubt it. If he thought this stuff was important, he wouldn't have left it lying out like that," Beth said. "Anyway, he probably makes the girls burn the trash, and they're not likely to tell him about our visit and that we probably took it, are they? Let's get out of here. I'd just as soon not be here when he gets back."

"Right behind you," Evie said.

Beth grabbed the bag and they ran back to the car. Evie sprinted ahead as they neared the car and opened the trunk. Beth threw in the trash bag, slammed the trunk, and they jumped into the car and took off, laughing as Evie peeled out of the driveway.

Evie went home to wait for her phone call. After a late lunch of a PB&J sandwich and milk, Beth settled down to investigate the trash bag that she'd dropped in front of the couch. Chestnut sat next to her, looking curiously at the contents as she withdrew them and sorted them onto the coffee table. She made a pile of battered movie magazines, searching for mailing labels. But there weren't any. Crystal must have bought them individually. There were also movie posters that had probably been ripped out of the magazines. Their edges were torn, and remnants of scotch tape clung to the edges, indicating they'd probably been taped to the walls of her bedroom.

Chestnut leaped onto the stack of magazines, scattering them, and then sliding over the edge with them before landing on the other side of the table.

"Chestnut, that's not helpful," Beth scolded.

He scampered away, hid under the bookcase, and glared at her as she gathered up the scattered pile. She took a closer look at the movie posters. They were mostly of recent movies: *The Graduate, Cool Hand Luke,* and *Bonnie & Clyde.* One was more weathered and yellowed than the others, and showed signs of multiple tapings, as though it had been moved over time. From *Dr. Zhivago,* it pictured two lead actors, Julie Christie and Omar Sharif, about to kiss.

Beth retrieved a couple of paper grocery bags from the kitchen to sort things into and then delved back into the trash bag. She pulled out, and discarded, nearly empty bottles of cosmetics and cheap perfumes, hairspray, curlers, broken 45s, an assortment of combs missing teeth, and matted brushes. There were a few old clothes, too tattered to be claimed by Sarah or Dawn, which Beth also discarded. All she knew, so far, was that, like most girls, Crystal liked movies, music, and getting dolled up. She had hoped to find some mail, a diary, or any type of written material that might provide a clue.

At the bottom of the bag, her hand closed on a hard square object. Was it a book? No, that wasn't it. It seemed to be some type of box. She withdrew the object. It was a battered wooden jewelry box, painted with an ivory background decorated with multicolored daisies. Beth opened it and a ballerina popped up in front of a triangle-shaped mirror, standing on a pink satin stage. The fabric also covered the inside of the box, which had just one compartment. Inside it was a single glass earring and a few beads from a broken bracelet or necklace. It looked like Sarah or Dawn had cleaned out whatever of value might have been inside. Beth closed the lid, turned it over, and twisted the winding key, and then turned it back over and reopened the lid. This time, the ballerina twirled in front of the mirror, while a tinny song played. Beth frowned in concentration and then nodded.

"It's Lara's Song, from Dr. Zhivago" she informed Chestnut, who had ventured out to examine the moving figure. "That movie must have been one of her favorites."

Chestnut cocked his head, as though considering it, and gingerly reached a paw toward the spinning ballerina.

"No, no, that's not a toy," Beth told him and snapped the lid shut.

As she turned the box sideways, she felt something shift inside. She held the box close to her ear and shook it. She heard something move inside. The earing and the beads rattled, but there was something else, a rustling sound. Curious, she reopened the music box.

The ballerina sprang back to life and twirled as the song played, slowed, and then stopped. Beth poked around inside and felt something give way under the floor of the interior compartment. She ran to the kitchen and returned with a butter knife. She pried out the bottom, a thin piece of balsa wood glued to the underside of the pink, satin fabric. Below was a small pile of papers. She picked them up and thumbed through them.

Beth gasped. Here were some clues, at last. There was an envelope addressed to Crystal, with a printed return address of the office of Mr. Frederick Nobis, Esq., a postcard with a picture of the Foshay Tower in Minneapolis, Minnesota, both with a post office box address, and a savings account book from the First National Bank of Davison City. She jumped up and ran to the phone, hanging on to the papers as she dialed Evie's number, only to get a busy signal. That's right, she would be on the phone with Jim right now. Beth would try back in a few minutes.

Beth sat down at the kitchen table and turned over the postcard. Written in a curly cursive hand, in blue ink, was a note that read, "Dear Chris (was that her nickname?), I am so happy to hear that you are planning to come to the cities. Let me know when to expect you, and I will meet you at the station. Looking forward to seeing you soon, Donna." The note wasn't dated but the postmark indicated that it had been mailed in early December.

It looked like maybe Crystal wasn't as friendless as Al thought. She seemed to have at least one friend. Maybe Chrystal had planned to visit Donna for Christmas, or maybe she had planned to leave Al for good and move to the cities.

Beth looked inside the envelope from Mr. Nobis. Disappointed, she found that there was nothing inside. *What had been in it?* she wondered. *And why did she save the envelope but not the letter?* She checked the postmark; it was also dated in early December. There had been something going on in Crystal's life. Something had changed.

Lastly, Beth picked up the savings account booklet. A first deposit of $20.00 was made in July, and she had made small deposits every week or two since. Beth wondered about that. Did Al know that she had a bank account and that she was adding to it? It seemed unlikely. If he wanted to keep her under his thumb, why allow her to have her own money? So, how was she managing it? Where did the money come from, and how did she get to the bank without Al, or the other working girls, knowing about it? Was this part of the special treatment that Sarah had complained about?

Beth ran a finger down the row of entries. Crystal's balance had grown, bit by bit, to over $200 by the end of November. Beth turned the page and whistled. Crystal had deposited $1,000 on December 9. She skipped down to the final entry. On December 20, the day before she died, Crystal had withdrawn the entire amount.

Beth tried calling Evie again, and this time she got through.

"You'll never guess what I found," Beth said.

"What?" Evie said. She sounded tired.

"Some clues. Really great clues. Can you come over?"

"I'll be right there," Evie said, her voice brighter.

Beth put the kettle on for tea. Chestnut heard her opening cupboards and came to investigate.

"This calls for a celebration," she said as she rummaged around in the cupboards and pulled a box of treats for him and a box of cookies for her and Evie.

"Meow," he agreed.

Chapter 14

Miss Tanner pulled the desk lamp closer and peered at the ring Beth had just handed her. She gasped, opened her top desk drawer, rooted around, and retrieved a magnifying glass.

"Oh, my. This is interesting," she said, turning it from side to side. "As I thought, it certainly appears to be an abraxas stone. The inscription might be Greek, but I'm not sure." She paused while she examined it. "I wonder, is it a genuine antique, or a copy?" She looked at Beth over the top of her horn-rimmed glasses. "This is the one you found near the railroad station, right?"

"That's right. We found it the day after I saw the girl's body—at least, I thought it was a body—roll down the hill."

"Yes, of course." Miss Tanner continued to examine the ring. Then she put the magnifying glass down on her desk. "I wonder if you might permit me to keep this for a few days. I know someone who has some expertise in antiquities, who might be able to tell us more about it."

"Well, I…" Beth trailed off and chewed the side of her lip. It might be a good idea to get Miss Tanner involved. Clearly, she knew people who might help. On the other hand, this wasn't part of the plan.

"Yes, what is it?"

"It's just that Evie and I decided we should turn it over to the police. You know, in case someone has reported it missing."

"Oh, I see. Well, we can soon clear that up." Miss Tanner pulled the phone over and dialed "O" for the operator and asked to be connected to the police. Once they rang her through, she explained who she was, provided a brief description of the ring, and inquired if anyone had reported one missing.

"No? I see. Just a moment, please." She placed a hand over the receiver. "They haven't gotten a report of a lost ring in the past couple of weeks. Would you like to have a policeman swing by and take a look at it, in case someone does report it?"

"I suppose that would be okay," Beth said.

She paused for a moment. Everything was happening so quickly that she felt a bit flustered. Miss Tanner had seized control and was making decisions. She had hoped to see Officer Crample at the station and ask what he'd found out about the license plate in the photograph. But, if he stopped by the library, maybe that would be a chance to ask him about it.

"Ask them to send over Bill Crample," she said. "He knows the most about it."

Miss Tanner relayed the message along with instructions about getting into the library through the side door since the workmen were still working on the front door. With a triumphant look, she hung up.

"There, all taken care of. They said they will radio his car, and that he should be here shortly. Please finish shelf reading that section you were working on last week while you listen for a knock on the side door, and then bring him up to my office when he arrives. Meanwhile, do you want this back?" She held out the ring.

"No, that's okay. Keep it and show it to your antiquities expert, unless Officer Crample says he needs to take it back to the station with him." Beth was relieved not to have it in her possession any longer. There was something sinister about it.

The loud knock on the library's side door startled Beth. She almost dropped the book she'd just pulled from the shelf. She replaced it sideways to mark where she'd stopped, and hurried to the door. She opened it to a rush of cold air and blindingly bright light from the sun reflecting off of the snow. Bill Crample stood there, his body angled sideways, looking off into the distance. Under the rim of his police cap, the tops of his ears were red from the cold.

"Come on in," she said as she stepped aside.

"Okay, nice-ta-see-ya," he mumbled, unsmiling, as he stepped inside and Beth shut the door behind him.

He seems out of sorts, Beth thought. *I suppose he was busy and was annoyed that he had to go out of his way.*

"Come on up to the librarian's office. She has that ring I found."

He just grunted and lumbered up the stairs after her. When they reached the main floor, he asked, "So you found a ring? When was this?"

"The day after I found the body," was all she said. She didn't want to go into a long explanation for the moment.

Miss Tanner was waiting with her office door open. She got to her feet as they approached, and smiled.

"Come in, won't you. Thank you for stopping by. I hope we didn't take you too far out of your way."

"No, that's okay. It's not a big town, so I'm never very far out of my way," he said, removing his hat and gloves.

Miss Tanner handed him the ring. "This is the item in question. Have a seat, won't you?" She waved them toward the chairs in front of her desk.

After they were all seated, Crample took a closer look at the ring. "So, Beth, you found this? Tell me about that." He continued to examine it as he listened to her story.

He glanced up when she stopped talking. "How did you know where to look?"

"We were checking out the scene of the crime."

Officer Crample suppressed a smile.

Beth continued, "Evie was at the top of the hill and I was at the bottom. I directed her to the spot where I'd seen the body…" She noticed him stiffen. "That is to say, the woman who fell down the hill. Anyway, I directed her to the spot and told her to wait there while I climbed up to meet her. When I got up there, she said she'd seen something shiny. So, we dug around in the snow and found this."

Crample looked up from the ring, his face impassive. "Just found it lying in the snow, huh? So, it could have been there for months, or even years, and not be related to anything that happened the night before."

"I guess so," she admitted, feeling her cheeks get hot.

"Okay. Well, it's an interesting bauble." He stood up and handed it back to Miss Tanner. "But no one has reported losing one."

"Then, you would have no objection if we hang on to it for the time being?" Miss Tanner asked.

"Nope, not at all. Finders' keepers, far as I'm concerned. If someone does report a lost ring, I know where it is. My guess is it's probably a cheap knock-off someone picked up at a flea market. Well, I better get back to work." He got up to leave and Beth trailed behind as he went back down the stairs.

As he approached the door, Beth said, "Just a minute, there's something else I wanted to talk to you about. If you have a few minutes."

He turned toward her, one hand on the doorknob. "Sure. What can I do for you?"

"The license plate."

"The what?" His face was blank.

"The license plate in the picture. Did you look it up?"

"Oh, that, right. Yeah, I did." He patted his pockets, wandered over to a table, put down his hat and gloves, and retrieved a little notebook from an inside jacket pocket. "I had the girls in dispatch look it up for me, as a sort of favor. You know." He winked at her, which Beth found very annoying.

"Okay, yup, here it is. I have a name and address to go with that plate." He ripped the page out of the notebook and handed it to her. "There you go. You owe me one."

"Thanks, I think," she said.

The name didn't mean anything to her. The address was in Grand Bend. But she'd check it out. It was a lead.

"Do you still have the picture? Can I have it back?"

"What for?"

Trying to keep her voice pleasant, she said, "To show to this person in Grand Bend. Anyway, why do you care? Why shouldn't I have it, since there's no case, as you keep reminding me?"

"Okay, okay. No need to get hysterical." He pulled out his wallet and fished out the picture of the girls and the car and handed it over to her.

"By the way, keep an eye out on your way home. I thought I saw Al's flashy purple car prowling around. In fact, why don't I pick you up and take you home? What time do you get off work?"

Beth was horrified by the thought of being driven home in a patrol car. That's all she needed to get every tongue in town wagging.

"Thanks for the warning, but, no thanks. I'll be fine. If I need a ride I'll call Evie or my dad."

"Suit yourself." He hemmed and hawed, but didn't have too much else to say. Finally, he said, "Well, I'd better get back to work, then." A few moments later, he left, and Beth made sure the door was securely locked behind him.

Chapter 15

After Beth finished shelf reading and dusting the first floor of the library, she went upstairs, tapped on Miss Tanner's office door, and stuck her head in.

"I've finished downstairs. I'm going out to lunch now. I'll start on the main floor when I get back."

"Perfect timing. The carpenters finished working on the front entrance this morning, so you won't have to put up with that racket. How much do you think you can get done this afternoon?" Miss Tanner asked.

"Maybe just the fiction collection." Beth had decided to work in the front of the library, rather than back in the nonfiction section, so she could keep an eye out for Al's car in case he was lurking around the library like Bill Crample said he was. "I'm sorry, but I won't be able to finish shelf reading this floor today."

"That's okay. I had a hunch that might happen. So, I put our high-school volunteers on notice. I'll give them a call." Miss Tanner sighed as she reached for the phone. "They aren't that accurate, and the constant giggling is something else." She shook her head and trailed off as she dialed. "On the plus side, they work for free and they can at least get the place dusted before we open to the public. I'll come in tomorrow and keep an eye on them. You should double-check their work on Thursday and Friday."

"I'm sorry," Beth said. "Are you sure you don't want me to come in tomorrow, too?"

"No, no, it's a holiday. You're entitled to have the day off." She turned away. "Hello," she said into the phone as she waved a dismissal toward Beth.

Beth shut the office door, quickly bundled up, and ran out the front door, through a cloud of fresh paint odor in the new entryway.

She'd brought a sandwich for her lunch, intending to stay in and read, but she'd changed her mind, deciding instead to run down to the bank. It was only a couple blocks away, and if Beverly, another of her high-school classmates, was working today, she might be able to convince her to divulge some information about Crystal's bank account. Beth was sure that Beverly would have noticed Crystal, a somewhat exotic-looking stranger.

A brisk walk got Beth to the bank. Even though it had only taken a few minutes, her cheeks stung from the cold. It felt nice to step into the warmth of the bank's lobby.

Great, Beverly was there, standing at a teller window doing something with a stamp pad. Her thin, blond hair stood out in frizzy curls around her head, and her blue eyes were magnified by the thick lenses of her glasses, giving her a permanently startled expression.

She looked up and smiled as Beth approached. "Hi, Beth, what brings you to the bank today?"

"I need to get a little cash since tomorrow is a holiday," Beth said.

Beverly slid a withdrawal slip across the counter.

As Beth started to fill it out, she said, trying to sound casual, "Say, since it's about lunchtime, how about we pop over to Woolworths for lunch, if you can get away?"

Beverly stared at her with a more than usually surprised expression. "Sorry, no. Mr. Brown is out to lunch. I have to stay here until he gets back."

"How about going out for coffee after work. What time do you get off?"

"Nope, sorry again. Mother is picking me up."

Beth slid the filled-out withdrawal slip back across the counter.

Beverly glanced at it. "Fives and ones okay?"

"Sure." Beth nodded.

Beverly counted out Beth's twenty-dollar withdrawal.

"So, why the sudden interest in getting together?" Beverly's magnified eyes narrowed in suspicion behind her glasses. "Usually, you hardly say 'hello' when you stop by the bank."

Beth felt her cheeks get hot, and she laughed nervously. "You got me. Actually, I was hoping to ask you a few questions."

Beverly smiled. "Don't be coy, just ask."

"It's about this girl." Beth rooted through her purse, found a photo of Crystal, and handed it over to Beverly. "Do you recall her coming into the bank the week before Christmas?"

Beverly squinted at it, and then looked up at Beth. "Does this have to do with the girl you saw roll down the hill in Central Park? A dead girl, or so they say."

"Yeah, but she's not dead. I guess she was just stunned, and now she's missing."

A loud throat-clearing alerted Beth to the woman waiting behind her.

Beth turned and said, "Oh, Sorry. I didn't see you there." Beverly handed the photo back to Beth.

Beth stepped aside, walked over to the check-writing counter, and stashed the cash and picture in her purse while waiting for Beverly to finish waiting on the other customer.

Outside, a splash of purple against the white background caught Beth's eye. An electric shock of fear shot through her, from head to toe, as she turned and watched Al's car slowly drive past the bank. So, it was true. Al was lurking around and watching her. She stood, rooted to the spot, unaware that the other customer had finished her business and left the bank.

Beverly called out, "Beth, did you want to ask me something?"

"Oh, yeah, sorry." She returned to the teller window. "So, did that girl—I think her name is Crystal Jones—come in the bank the week before Christmas?"

Beverly wrinkled her brow. "Yeah, I think so. She comes in pretty often. I didn't wait on her. I think that time she came in to talk to Mr. Brown. Why do you ask?"

Beth stopped and thought, *that's a good question. Why do I ask? Why do I care so much?*

She said, "Just curious, I guess. I may have been the last person who saw her before she disappeared. I just want to track her down and find out if she's okay or, if not, find out what happened to her."

Beverly regarded her with a skeptical smile. "You always were kind of the Nancy Drew wannabe. Weren't you?"

Beth forced a laugh, going along with the joke, but remembering why she never really liked Beverly, the sarcastic little so-and-so.

"Something like that. So, what can you tell me about Crystal? How often did she come in? When was she last in? What was she doing the last time she was here?"

"Whoa, that's a lot of questions. I don't know how much I should divulge." Beverly picked up a pencil and tapped the eraser end against the counter as she thought. "Tell you what, do me a favor and I'll see what I can dig up."

"Favor? What kind of favor?"

"You know Sam."

"Sam?"

"Yeah, you know, Sam Daniels. He works for your brother."

"Oh, yeah, that Sam. What about him?"

"Well, I'd kind of like to go out with him, but I don't know how to get his attention."

"Really?"

"Yeah, I've had a crush on him since we were in middle school. Didn't you know?"

"No, sorry, I didn't have a clue. I guess you hid it well."

"Huh, yeah, maybe too well. Anyway, if you can get him to ask me out, I'll spill the details." She scribbled on a scrap of paper and pushed the note, with her name and phone number on it, across to Beth. "Deal?"

"No promises, but I'll see what I can do. When do you think you can get me that information?"

"I'll make notes of anything I can think of that might help you today, and I'll give you a call after I hear from Sam."

"Okay, thanks."

Before leaving the bank, Beth stuck her head out the door and, after looking both ways and not seeing Al's car, she ran back to the library.

As she worked, Beth glanced out of the library windows repeatedly, but she didn't see Al's purple car. Maybe it was a coincidence that he had passed the bank when she was there.

As the afternoon wore on, she stopped looking and was startled by the sound of a car honking outside. She ran to the window and was relieved to see Evie's car parked in front of the building. Good, she had a ride home. They had planned that Evie would pick her up after work if she got back to town in time. Beth said goodbye to Miss Tanner and hurried out the front door and down the steps.

Once in the car, she said, "Thanks for picking me up. Wow, it's nice and warm in here. Did you just get back from Grand Bend?"

"Yes. You wouldn't believe the day I had. I stood in line for ages to get a drop-add form. Then, I chased around for the prof to get his signature. Then, back to another line to register for the class. What an ordeal. But now it's done. How was your day?"

"Interesting. Do you have time for a cup of tea? I'll tell you all about it."

"Sure. I'm parched, and tea sounds great."

As they entered Beth's house, Chestnut acknowledged their greetings with one half-opened eye and a yawn, and then curled back up on the sofa to finish his nap as the girls went through to the kitchen.

"Do you have any more of your mom's Christmas cookies?" Evie asked while peeking into Beth's cupboards.

"Nope, sorry. They don't last too long around here. We'll have to make do with graham crackers and peanut butter," Beth said.

"Oh, yum. I'll add some honey to mine." Evie rooted around and collected the ingredients, plates, and silverware that they needed for their snack, while Beth made the tea. Soon, they were sipping and nibbling while Beth filled Evie in on the latest news about her trip to the bank and conversation with Beverly.

Then Beth pulled out Crystal's bankbook, the envelope from the lawyer, Mr. Nobis, and the postcard that she had found in the jewelry box, and laid them on the table so they could take another look at them.

"Crystal must have thought this stuff was important and she wanted to keep it secret. Obviously, the bankbook is important. I can't imagine that Al would want her to accumulate funds allowing her to get away from him. I'm not so sure about the significance of the other two items."

Evie picked up and read the postcard.

"It looks like we were right. Crystal was planning to go to the cities and she'd contacted someone telling them she was coming. Assuming she's the Chris that this postcard is addressed to, and if this is her post office box."

Evie compared the address on the postcard to the address on the envelope from the lawyer addressed to Crystal Jones.

"These are addressed to the same P.O. box number. So, yeah, I guess Crystal and Chris are the same person."

She stopped and wrinkled her forehead in thought as she added another dab of peanut butter and a drop of honey to a graham cracker.

"I wonder where the key is."

"The key to the post office box? That's a good question," Beth said. "I didn't find one." She paused to think as she stirred her tea. "Without the key, we'll probably never get to see what else might be in that box."

Evie picked up the envelope. "And this is kind of weird. Why keep an empty envelope?"

"I know. It's another mystery. We could ask Mr. Nobis, but how? What would be our excuse for wanting to know, and would he tell us? Speaking of getting information, I forgot the best part. You'll never guess what Beverly said when I asked her for information on Crystal."

"What?"

"She likes Sam Daniels and will trade information on Crystal for a date with him if I can set them up."

"No way. You have got to be kidding. Her and Sam?" Evie burst out laughing.

"I kid you not. According to her, she's had a crush on him since middle school. She gave me her name and number and said that if I get him to call and ask her out, she'll spill the beans on all she knows about Crystal's dealings with the bank."

"Oh, no. Can you even picture the two of them together?" Evie said.

They both laughed at the thought until tears ran down their cheeks.

Once she caught her breath, Beth said, "Stranger couples have happened. The question is, how do we convince him to ask her out in the first place? And, should I? I can just picture it. If they get together she'll sit at home trying to balance the checkbook while he runs around. Poor Beverly."

"Don't overthink it. It's just a date. Who knows if they'll even hit it off? And, if they do, who are we to stand in the way of true love?" Evie stifled another fit of giggles.

"As far as how to convince him, that's easy. He's always so broke, he'd do anything for a few bucks. If we pay for the date, I bet he'll be willing."

"That's a thought," Beth said. "Well, I need to go to Gary's garage to get my car before school starts next week. His shop will be closed tomorrow, but I was going to ask Gary to take me over there and pick up my car, assuming it's ready. But I suppose I could wait until Thursday or Friday instead, and go in the evening when Sam's around. If you're willing to haul me around for another day or two."

"Not a problem."

"Speaking of driving me places. How do you feel about driving to Grand Bend tomorrow to try and track down the owner of the car that Crample looked up, and see if she can tell us more about Crystal?"

Beth retrieved her purse, pulled out the slip of paper Bill Crample had torn out of his notebook and handed it to Evie.

"Sure, it sounds like an adventure." Evie glanced at the clock on Beth's wall. "Oh jeez, is that the time? I'd better get going. I'll see you tomorrow."

Chapter 16

Today was the first day of 1969. New Year's was a holy day and Beth had gone to mass with her family. Her dad, mom, and sister had picked her up and then they had met her brother, Gary, and her sister-in-law, Debbie, at the church. However, Beth let them know she had plans with Evie, so she wouldn't be able to join them for the usual midday ham dinner that marked the end of the holidays for the Williams family.

After mass, when the rest of the family stopped in the vestibule to chat with Father McClure, Beth excused herself and went back up to the front of the church, to the Holy Mother's side altar. She dropped a quarter in the offering box, lit a vigil light, and said a quick prayer for the repose of the soul of Crystal Jones.

When she walked back to join her family, Father McClure was gone and the rest of them were standing in a cluster, heads down, talking. They stopped talking and watched her as she approached. Debbie looked upset, Gary looked annoyed, her parents and sister just looked a little confused.

"Why did you tell Father McClure that Debbie wanted to become Catholic?" Gary demanded when she joined them.

"I didn't…that is…I don't think I did. Is that what he said?" Beth said.

"Yes, and it was very embarrassing for Debbie."

"It's okay, Gary. It's not that important," Debbie said.

"If you didn't say it, then why did he think you did?" Gary asked.

"Let me think…" Beth hesitated as she tried to recall what she'd said to Father McClure when she and Evie had talked to him. "I may have said something about someone wanting to become Catholic. I guess he jumped to a wrong conclusion." She turned to Debbie. "I'm sorry, Debbie. I didn't mean to put you on the spot."

"But, who did you mean?" Gary said.

"Oh, leave your sister alone," Dad interrupted. "I'm sure she meant well. Anyway, we need to get home. Mother will want to put that ham in the oven. Are you sure you can't join us?" He asked Beth.

"I wish I could, but Evie and I are going to Grand Bend. Is it okay if I stop by later for a snack after we get back?" Beth asked her mother.

"Of course, dear. You know you're always welcome," her mother said.

Beth wound her scarf around her neck.

"I'll talk to you later, Gary, and explain everything. And I want to ask you about my car, too. Okay?"

"Your car is ready if that's what you want to know," Gary said. He sounded annoyed.

"Great," Beth said, ignoring the subtext. "Well, gotta run. Evie's waiting. See you all later."

As Beth and Evie drove to Grand Bend, snow restlessly wove across the highway, driven by the unceasing westerly winds that blew across the vast expanses of the prairies of eastern Montana and North Dakota, and into northwestern Minnesota. It was a rare day when the wind didn't blow, and the few spindly trees, bare now in the January gloom, did little to slow it down. Periodically, a gust would lift the dry snow off the surrounding fields and swirl it around their car. Then, Evie had to slow down and watch for snatches of the painted centerline to stay on the highway.

The first indication they were close to East Grand Bend was the big factory on the outskirts of the city, surrounded by heaps of sugar beets that were partially covered by snow, sitting in an open field. Smokestacks poured smoke into the leaden sky.

"Boy, I'm glad I left my job in the Davison City sugar beet plant," Evie remarked as they drove past. "A few more years in that place, and I'd have been brain dead."

East Grand Bend, Minnesota, sat on the east side of the river that divided the smaller Minnesota city from Grand Bend, North Dakota. On the outskirts of town, they passed gas stations, storage buildings, warehouses, and factories, which sheltered them from the open winds and made driving easier.

"Where, exactly, are we headed?" Evie asked.

"131 Water Street, Grand Bend," Beth said. "If I recall correctly, the street follows the river. Cross the bridge and then take the first right turn."

"That must not be a great address in the spring," Evie said.

"That's for sure," Beth said.

Soon, they arrived at the address, a gray slat-board-sided house with a crumbling front sidewalk. At least it was across the street from the river, and sitting atop a small hillock, providing some protection from the almost annual spring floods.

They parked and walked up the path. Beth pushed the doorbell, then waited, but didn't hear anything inside.

Perhaps the doorbell was out of order, she thought. It looked like it had been painted over several times. She knocked, waited with teeth clenched against chattering in the cold, and then knocked again, more loudly.

"Yes, yes, I'm coming," came a voice from inside. It sounded like an older woman, not the younger voice of Crystal's friend that she'd expected.

She heard sounds of footsteps and locks turning. The door opened a crack—the chain lock was still on. A small woman with her hair in curlers and wearing a housecoat peered up at Beth.

"What do you want?" she asked, scowling.

"We'd like to see Rosemary. Is she home?"

"Oh her. I have no idea. They come and go at all hours. Go around to the side and knock," she said and then closed the door abruptly.

"Jeez! She's not very friendly," Beth said.

"That's an understatement," Evie said.

They followed a partially shoveled, trampled path around to a side door, and knocked. This time, the response was quicker. A short girl, with an untidy brown ponytail and a friendly smile, flung the door open. She carried a baby girl on one hip. The child, approximately a year old, wore only a diaper and t-shirt.

"Hi. Can I help you?" she said

"Are you Rosemary Simons?" Beth said.

"Yes, I am," she wrinkled her forehead, as though in thought. "Should I know you? I'm so bad at remembering people."

"You don't know us. We're friends of Crystal Jones," Beth said. "Can we come inside and talk?" The baby turned her face away from Beth and Evie and clung tightly to her mom's side. "It looks like your baby is cold."

"Friends of Crystal? Oh sure, sure. Come on in." She led them down the stairs into the living room area of an apartment. She stepped across toys that were strewn across an ancient brown carpet.

"Sorry about the mess. Have a seat," she said, waving them toward the worn brown and orange plaid sofa as she put the baby down on the floor. The baby quickly got up on her hands and knees, crawled over to a plastic block, picked it up, stuck it in her mouth, and started to gnaw on it.

"Thanks," Beth and Evie both said in tandem. This made them laugh, which startled the baby, who looked at them and then also laughed, a cute little high-pitched sound, which made all of the women laugh.

Beth and Evie removed their outerwear and took a seat. Rosemary sat in the matching chair arranged at a 90-degree angle with the couch.

"So, you're friends of Crystal. How is she?"

Evie and Beth looked at each other.

"Well, I'm not a friend, per se," Evie said.

"Actually, I don't know her, either," Beth said. "I only met her—well, saw her—one time."

Rosemary looked at them with a confused expression. "So then, what brings you here? What is it you want to know?"

"Let me explain," Beth said. She opened her purse and started to dig through it. "I found this picture." She produced the picture of Crystal and Rosemary leaning against a car and handed it to her. "Do you remember being in this picture?"

As Rosemary looked at it, a faraway smile dawned. "Oh, yeah. That was a great day. I'd just gotten my driver's license, and I'd gotten straight A's on my last report card. So, our foster parents signed over their old car to me. I still have it."

"You said 'our foster parents.' Does that mean you and Crystal were foster sisters?" Beth asked.

"Yes, that's right," Rosemary said.

"You still have the car. Is it outside? I didn't notice it," Beth said.

"No, John—that's my husband—drove it to work." She glanced at the narrow gold wedding ring on her left hand. "He works at the sugar beet plant. But, he also is taking classes when we can afford them. He's such a hard worker." She smiled, proudly.

Beth and Evie smiled back at her.

"Oh yes, we came from Davison City and passed the plant on our way into town," Evie said.

The baby crawled over to the couch and pulled herself up on unsteady legs. Hanging on, she sidled over toward Evie and, while clinging to the edge of the couch, smiled up at her, showing off her new, little teeth in her pink gums.

"This is Jenny," Rosemary said.

"Hi, Jenny," Evie said. "She's just darling. How old is she?"

"She'll be one year old next month," Rosemary said. "Oh, where are my manners. I should offer you something. I think I have some instant coffee. Would you like some?"

"Oh, we don't want to put you out," Beth said.

"Not at all. I was just about to make it, anyway."

"Well, if you're sure, let me help," Beth said.

"None for me, thanks," Evie said. "I'll stay here and keep an eye on Jenny."

Rosemary handed the photograph back to Beth and led her to the kitchen. "Have a seat. This will take a few minutes," she said.

Beth sat down at the kitchen table. The floral, oilcloth tablecloth provided a note of color in the small, windowless room. Rosemary filled a tea kettle and got out the mugs, spoons, and coffee crystals.

"You were saying that you saw Crystal. Gosh, I haven't seen her in such a long time. How is she?"

"Well...here's the thing...I think she's missing."

Rosemary sat down, across the table from Beth, and Beth told her about what had happened in the park—Crample's version.

Beth finished, "So, she's vanished. It looks like I might have been the last person to see her. I'm trying to locate her. Do you know where she might have gone?"

"Back to her boyfriend, I guess," she said, grimacing. "That Allen Peterson." She spat out his name.

"Oh, so you know Allen."

"Yes. We know him, all right."

"It sounds like you don't think too highly of him."

"No, I don't. We tried to tell her he was no good. I mean, me and our foster parents. But, he turned her head with stories about how they were going to strike it rich, and he talked her into running away with him."

"When was this?" Beth asked.

"A couple of years ago, I guess. She always had her head full of ideas about getting into the movies." She smiled, sadly. "She was a big movie fan. Every time she had a few dollars she spent it on movies and movie magazines. I don't think it went too well for her. She didn't keep in touch after that."

The teakettle whistled. They interrupted their conversation while they prepared their coffee and carried it back into the living room. Evie was on the floor playing with Jenny. She handed the baby toys. She took them, tasted them, banged them on the floor, and then discarded them.

"It looks like you have a new friend," Beth said to Evie.

Yes, Jenny is my widdle friend, aren't you?" Evie said, using baby talk as she reached out and tickled the baby's tummy, causing her to giggle.

"She doesn't usually take to strangers, but she seems to like you," Rosemary said.

Beth and Rosemary sat down. Evie got up off the floor and joined them.

"Rosemary and I were just talking about Crystal's boyfriend, Allen," Beth said to Evie. Turning to Rosemary she said, "Evie and I met him."

"You did? So he's still around. He never did take Crystal to Hollywood?"

"Probably not. Yes, he's around," Beth said.

"I take it that Crystal wasn't with him."

"No. But that's where we got the photo, and some of her other stuff, including movie magazines. So, I guess she's still a big fan. You mentioned foster parents, so you and Crystal lived together in a foster family?"

"Uh-huh, with Mr. and Mrs. Albert Johnson. They were almost like real parents to me, and we're still close. Although, we don't see them as often since they moved to the cities. I lived with them for six years, from the age of twelve until I finished high school. We're about the same age, Crystal and me, but Crystal came later. She was almost sixteen when she came and was almost eighteen years old when she left."

"Do you think that she is with your foster parents?" Crystal asked.

"No, I'm sure she's not. I just talked to them this morning. They were so upset when Crystal ran off, and about how she never contacted them afterward, so I'm sure they'd have told me if Crystal was there or had been in touch."

Soon, the baby fell asleep amid her toys, and Beth and Evie said it was time to go. Before they left, Rosemary wrote down her foster parents' phone number and address, and her own phone number, and Beth and Evie promised to stay in touch and let her know anything they found out about Crystal's whereabouts.

Chapter 17

As they approached Davison City, Evie said, "I see the Big Boy restaurant ahead. Did you ever hear back from that waitress, Sally?"

"No, she hasn't called and she was sick the last time we stopped in. When was that?" Beth said.

"Saturday. Remember? After we staked out the place and then chased that car."

"Right. That was really something."

"Should we stop in and see if she's working, now?"

"Sure, why not."

Evie parked and they went in. As they'd hoped, Sally was working, so they sat in a booth in her section. They examined the menus that had been propped up behind the condiments.

"I'll just have coffee," Beth said. "From here, I'm going to my parent's house, and my mom will be disappointed if I'm not hungry."

"Lucky you. I love your mom's cooking."

"You can come with me."

"Thanks, but I need to get home. Besides, I'm starving. I'm going to have a burger and fries. If you don't mind watching while I eat, I'll share my fries with you," Evie said.

"No, I don't mind," Beth said.

Sally came to take their order.

"Hi Sally, are you feeling better?" Beth said.

"What?"

"We stopped in on Saturday, and they said you were out sick."

"Oh yeah, right, I forgot," Sally said, with a giggle.

Beth guessed that meant the so-called "sickness" had been an excuse for time off from work.

"What are you going to have?" Sally poised a pencil over the order pad.

"I'll have a burger, fries, and a Coke," Evie said.

"And I'll just have a cup of coffee," Beth said. "Before you go, Sally, do you have a second?"

"Sure, what's up?"

"Did you get a chance to ask the rest of the staff if they noticed cars picking up Crystal or any other girls?"

Sally glanced over her shoulder in both directions, leaned in, dropped her voice, and said, "I'm not supposed to talk about it."

Beth was surprised by Sally's reaction. She looked around to see if anyone was watching, or if someone nearby might be listening in. No one was. It was the middle of the afternoon, and there were very few other diners.

"Really? Why's that?"

"I don't know," Sally said in the same hushed voice. "But, my boss got mad when he overheard me asking the kitchen staff about it, and I don't want to get into any more trouble."

As a customer approached the front cash register, a burly man in a suit came out of the backroom to accept his payment.

When she saw him, Sally straightened up and repeated their order in a normal tone of voice,

"A burger, fries, and a Coke here, and just coffee for you?" she said and then hurried off.

"That was kind of weird," Evie said. "Did you see how she reacted when that man came out of the kitchen? He's the manager, I suppose?"

"Yeah, must be. She seemed scared. I wonder why he would care if she asked around about cars picking up girls," Beth said.

"I don't know. It could be that he doesn't want her wasting time, or bothering the kitchen staff when she should be working," Evie said.

"Possibly. Or, if she calls in sick a lot and leaves them short-staffed, he has her pegged as a goof-off and is keeping a close eye on her." Beth paused and then said, "Or, maybe…he could have an arrangement with Allen."

"An arrangement? Like what?"

"Allen might be paying him to use this as a drop-off spot, and the manager doesn't want Sally calling attention to it."

Soon, Sally returned with their drinks. She glanced back toward the kitchen and then said, again in low tones, "Before Mr. Big Shot butted in, the cook said that this has been going on for a while, almost a year. Different cars, but always on Saturday nights. She held a finger up to her lips. "But, don't tell anyone that I told you, or I'll be looking for a new job."

Evie and Beth promised they wouldn't tell.

After she left, Beth said, "I guess we'll have to give her a big tip for that. But, I'm not sure if it helps us with our investigation. It seems like there must have been an arrangement or understanding of some sort."

"Right, and judging by last Saturday night, whatever was going on is still going on. So, it wasn't just something to do with Crystal."

"Poor Crystal," Beth said, suddenly feeling very sad for her. "She got a raw deal. Allen, that rat. He made promises and told her stories about taking her to Hollywood, and she bought it. If only she'd had sense enough to stay with her foster family."

"I know. Girls that age are dumb," Evie said.

Beth smiled at Evie's air of wisdom. "Yeah, we were dumb kids, too. We're much older and wiser now. Anyway, I guess we should contact the foster parents and verify that Crystal was planning a visit. It seems like she was. The stationmaster sold her a ticket to the cities. And, from the postcard, it seems clear someone was planning to pick her up when she got there."

"True. But, we don't know if that postcard is from her foster mom. It just had a first name on it. Donna, wasn't it? Do we know her foster mom's first name?" Evie said.

"Good question." Beth dug the slip of paper Rosemary had given her out of her purse. "Nope. It just says, Mr. and Mrs. Albert Johnson. We should have asked Rosemary, I guess."

"Also, Rosemary said her foster parents would have let her know if Crystal had been in touch with them," Evie said.

"You're right. The postcard might be from someone else in the cities. I should talk to the Johnsons and find out. I can't go down there. I don't have the time or the money to make an overnight trip. I guess I'll call," Beth said.

"Yeah, and we only have a few days left before the next quarter starts, and I still have to buy my textbooks."

"Okay, here's the plan. I'll call them later tonight to let them know who we are and that I'm looking for Crystal. I'll ask them if they know who Donna is and to call me if they hear anything useful. I'll let you know what I find out."

Sally brought the plate with the hamburger and fries.

Evie positioned the plate so the French fries were close to Beth.

"Have some. It's more than I can eat," she said as she applied ketchup and mustard to her burger and put a blob of ketchup next to the fries. "By the way, maybe I should approach Sam Daniels about dating Beverly, instead of you."

"Sure, if you want to. But, why?" Beth said. She picked up a fry, dipped it into the ketchup, popped it into her mouth, and savored the greasy, salty flavor.

"Well, he had a thing for me. So maybe I can get him to ask Beverly out without bribing him. Neither one of us has a lot of money to throw around. Anyway, you have to work. I don't. And I want to help solve the case."

"Great. I'll make the phone calls, you try to set up Sam and Beverly, and then we'll compare notes. Do you want to come over to my place tomorrow after work?"

"Sure. You know what, Beth?"

"Don't say it."

"I think the game's afoot."

"Oh no. You said it."

Beth leaned against the counter in her mom's kitchen and watched as her mother prepared a ham sandwich for her.

"Are you getting enough to eat now that you're living on your own?" her mom asked.

"I sure am. Especially during the holidays." Beth patted her tummy. "Once school starts, I'm going on a diet."

"Don't be silly. You're just the right size," Mom said. "You will need to keep up your strength for your studies."

Beth smiled at her mom's repetition of her belief that mental work was more taxing than physical work. She had given up trying to convince her she was wrong about that.

"Well, I'm glad you think I'm the right size, but I certainly don't look like Twiggy or the other girls in the fashion magazines."

"And why should you? They're nothing but skin and bone. One strong wind would blow them away. You look healthy."

Beth took her sandwich to the kitchen table, got a bottle of Tab out of the fridge, and sat down with her sister, Cathy, who was flipping through the Sears catalog. Mom dished up slices of pie and then joined them.

Cathy pushed the catalog over to Beth. "What do you think of this outfit?"

"Cute," Beth said. "But don't you already have a closet full of things you haven't worn?"

Cathy stuck her tongue out at her sister, tucked the catalog under her arm, and said, "I'm going to ask Debbie," and went downstairs.

"Yum, lemon meringue," Beth said, eyeing her slice. "You make the best pies, Mom."

"I know," her mom said, and they both laughed. "I could teach you how to make one."

"That would be great. But maybe I should start with something easier, like oatmeal raisin cookies. Those are the best. Of course, it would help if I owned a cookie sheet."

"I have too many. You can have one of mine."

They were discussing recipes when the basement door opened and Gary came up, out of the rec room.

"Hi Beth," he said. "I thought I heard your voice. Debbie and Cathy are talking about clothes, and Dad is asleep in front of the TV, so I came up to join you." He helped himself to a slice of pie and a soft drink and sat down.

"When do you want to go pick up your car?" he asked Beth between forkfuls.

"Is it good to go?"

"Yup, ready when you are. We can go over there now, if you want to."

"I guess we can, once I finish eating and help Mom clean up."

"Oh, don't worry about that. I'll take care of it. It's just a few dishes. You kids run along." Turning to Beth, she said, "I'll send over a baking sheet and the cookie recipe with Debbie and Gary. They can drop it by your place on their way home."

Beth went downstairs and said hello to Debbie and, a few minutes later, she and Gary were on their way to the repair shop.

"What's the deal with the whole Debbie becoming Catholic stuff?" he asked. "I know it bothers her to feel pressured like that."

"I didn't say it was her. I thought about it, and I'm sure I said 'a friend' was thinking about converting. So, I don't know where Father McClure got that. He probably just made it up. You know how he likes to exaggerate."

"Yeah, okay. But why would you tell him anything like that? Is this part of your sleuthing?"

"Kind of. I needed an excuse to talk to him."

"Is he a suspect?"

"No, he's not a suspect, not really. But, he was late to Saturday evening mass the night Crystal died, and I wondered why. He went off on one of his story-telling tangents, so we didn't find out anything."

"That sounds like him." Gary stopped to think, and then said, "Beth, I wish you wouldn't get involved with this. Just let it go. That girl was involved with some unsavory types."

"Unsavory? How would you know that? Is there something you're not saying?"

"Oh, for God's sake. No. Nothing like that. I just don't think a nice girl would stand around in a parking lot and get picked up by someone old enough to be her father."

"The banker, right?"

"Yeah, the banker. Well, you know what I mean. She wasn't in a nice business, and dealt with all types."

"True, but you know what? I met her foster sister earlier today, and she's a nice person. Maybe Crystal was nice, too, until she fell in with the wrong people. I have to find out what happened to her. If someone killed her, I don't want that person around and maybe hurting another girl. I can't let it go. Please don't tell anyone, especially Mom and Dad."

They turned into Dave's Auto Repairs.

"Okay, I won't," he said, reluctantly. "But, be careful and let me know if you need my help."

Dave's Auto Repair was locked up and deserted on this holiday evening, but Gary went in and soon pulled out with her freshly washed and waxed car. Soon, Beth was behind the wheel of the 1963 Chevy Impala that her grandma had given her when she bought a newer model, what she fondly thought of as her Batmobile, and sailing down the street on her way home.

Driving felt odd after being without her wheels for most of the past two weeks. It would be nice to come and go as she pleased and not have to depend on others for rides. She parked in her spot behind the duplex and reminded herself to plug in the engine block heater so it would start in the morning since her rent didn't include a spot in the garage.

Beth went into the back porch to retrieve the extension cord. When she came back out, she thought she saw the tail end of a purple car drive slowly down the alley behind the garage.

Was it Al's car? Was he stalking her? Her heart started to beat faster. What did he want?

She dropped the extension cord and ran to the alley to see if she could get a better look. It was late afternoon and already dark, but as the slow-moving car drove under a streetlight near the end of the alley, she thought it looked like his car. A shot of fear ran through her body, and she stood there, shaking and breathing hard as she stared after it for a moment, before she turned back toward her duplex, plugged in the engine block heater, and went inside.

Chestnut came to greet her as she opened the back door into the kitchen, hopped up on the table, and looked up at her, meowing for a treat.

"Oh Chestnut, sometimes I wish you were a big mean dog instead of a cat," she said as she removed the gloves from her clammy hands and scratched behind his ears. He began to purr and seemed to smile.

Chestnut trailed behind her as she turned the deadbolt locks on the front and back doors, pulled the shades, and closed the curtains, before taking off her winter wraps.

"It was probably someone else in that car. I'm just over-reacting," she told him. Then, she got out the kitty treats and put on the kettle.

A little later, a loud knock on her front door startled her. Hesitating, her hand on the lock, she called out, "Who is it?"

"It's me, Gary."

Beth opened the door and he was standing in the door holding a cookie sheet with a piece of folded, lined paper taped to it. Behind him, his truck was parked with the motor running.

"Mom sent this over." He handed her the cookie sheet. "Who were you expecting?"

"No one. Do you want to come in for a while?" she asked, trying not to sound too eager.

"No, we need to get home. Debbie is tired," he said, gesturing to the truck. "Are you okay? You seem a little jumpy."

"Yeah, I'm fine. I guess I forgot you were going to stop by. Thanks for this," she said, raising the pan.

"No problem. Did your car work okay on the way home? Did you remember to plug it in?"

"Yup, worked good, and yes, I did plug it in."

"Great. Okay then, we'll see you soon." He turned, then stopped and came back.

"One thing I've been meaning to tell you. You know that black Pontiac you asked me about?"

"You mean the one Evie and I followed?"

"Yup."

"What about it?"

"It's weird because it couldn't have been that car. It was in the shop."

"I thought you said you'd worked on it earlier that week. Not that it was still in the shop."

"Yeah, I said that, but then I remembered Mr. Gloor was slow about picking it up. He didn't pick it up until after you saw it out at the Big Boy. So he couldn't have been driving it. Unless, for some reason, he came and got it and returned it later that night. But, that doesn't make sense. I'll ask Sam about it... Anyway, gotta go." He hurried back to his pick-up.

Beth relocked the door, turned on the TV, and popped a TV dinner into the oven. The calming voice of Walter Cronkite soon filled her apartment while she tried to puzzle out this latest development and plan her phone call to Crystal's foster parents.

Chapter 18

January 2, 1969

Miss Tanner clattered to the circulation desk with a stack of book catalogs.

"You can go to lunch, now, Miss Williams," she announced.

Beth dashed out of the library and drove to the Piggly Wiggly. She had to start the car, anyway, or it might not start after work, after sitting in the cold for eight hours. Besides, Evie was coming over after supper, and she wanted to surprise her with some homemade oatmeal cookies.

Clutching her mom's cookie recipe, she grabbed a cart and raced up and down the aisles. She needed flour, nutmeg, baking soda—was that the square box or the round one? She put both in the cart, she'd figure it out later—and vanilla. She probably should get more brown sugar, butter, and raisins. Did she need one of those little pastry brushes her mom used to grease pans? She glanced around but didn't see one. She decided to improvise. Finally, she ran to the frozen foods aisle and threw a couple of her favorite Swanson TV dinners into the cart. They'd stay frozen in the trunk of her car until she went home.

As she turned her cart around, she saw Mr. Nobis walking toward her.

"Oh, hello there Miss, ah…"

"Miss Williams," she said.

"Oh, yes, of course. The girl from the library. I see you have some frozen dinners. Would you recommend that brand?"

"Well, I like them."

"I'm a bit out of my depth. My wife usually does the grocery shopping, but she is out of town visiting her mother. I'm batching it," he said, followed by an inauthentic laugh.

Beth said, "These are pretty good, but they're all kind of the same. It depends on what you want to eat."

"Of course." Mr. Nobis gazed into the middle distance, as though thinking of something else. Suddenly, he said, "I heard that you are looking for a young lady who has gone missing. Is that the case?"

Beth hesitated for a moment. Then decided on a direct course.

"Yes, that's true. Did you know Crystal?"

"Know her? No, I wouldn't say I knew her. Why do you ask?"

He wandered over to the freezer case and looked over the contents. Beth trailed behind him.

"Because you sent her a letter."

Mr. Nobis turned toward Beth, clutching a frozen chicken and dumplings dinner in one hand.

"How do you know that?"

"I saw it. Officer Crample took me out to...to where Crystal was living. He wanted me to identify her as the girl I saw fall down the hill, but she wasn't there. I identified her from a picture, and I saw some of the things in her room."

She left out the part about going back to Al's with Evie, and how she found the hidden envelope but not its contents.

"So, you know about the inheritance," he said.

"Oh yes, the inheritance." She tried to sound nonchalant, hoping that he would say more.

Mr. Nobis stared at her suspiciously and tossed the frozen dinner into his cart, turned away, and continued to browse the freezer section, grabbed a couple more packages, and dropped them into his cart.

"Perhaps this is not the best place to talk about this. Come to my office, if you wish to pursue the matter further. What time do you get off of work?"

"Four o'clock," she said.

"I assume you know where my office is on Main Street?"

Beth nodded. "Yes."

"I'll expect you shortly after four, then," he said, and then walked away.

Beth stood there for a moment, puzzling over this sudden twist. Then she shook her head and checked her watch. Her lunch break would be over soon. Luckily, she had her car, which would save time, and make getting all this stuff home easier.

The sales clerk seemed to punch each price into the cash register at a sloth's pace, and the carry-out boy moved in slow motion as he put on his parka and gloves, before shuffling out to her car with her order. Still, she managed to make it back to the library with enough time to run down to the workroom and devour the cheese sandwich she'd brought for her lunch, and make it back upstairs to the circulation desk on time.

Miss Tanner adjusted her glasses and glanced at the clock before she looked at Beth and smiled approvingly at her promptness. As she gathered up her catalogs and pens, she said, "Would you and your friend, Evie, be free on Saturday morning? I hope you will be able to drop by my house around ten. My friend, the antiquities expert, would like to meet both of you and discuss the ring."

"I can. I'll ask Evie. She's coming over tonight," Beth said.

"Wonderful." Miss Tanner scribbled something on a piece of paper and handed it to Beth. "Here's my address. I hope to see both of you on Saturday."

Beth climbed the stairs to Mr. Nobis' second-floor office over the hardware store on Main Street. She'd puzzled over the reason for his requesting a visit with her all afternoon as she worked. What was in the letter that he'd sent to Crystal, and what was his interest in her? She still hadn't come up with any answers.

She stopped on the landing to catch her breath before opening the door with his name emblazoned in black lettering on the opaque glass window. She entered an empty outer office. Apparently, his secretary had left for the day. A small wooden desk with a phone, a covered typewriter, and stacked piles of folders faced the door. The door to the inner office was ajar.

As Beth approached, Mr. Nobis stood up and smiled.

"Good. You made it. Thank you for coming. Won't you have a seat?" He gestured toward one of the two chairs sitting facing his desk. "Can I get you anything; water or coffee, perhaps?"

"No, no thank you." She sat down and glanced around the small, wood-paneled office, and the framed diplomas on the wall behind his desk. "I don't have much time. I'm expecting a friend later this evening."

"Of course." He sat and leaned back in his swivel chair.

His heavy-lidded eyes didn't reveal much, but Beth guessed that when she said "friend" he assumed she meant a boyfriend. She waited for him to start the conversation. After all, she was here at his invitation.

"You mentioned finding a letter," he said.

"Yes, to Crystal from your office. About an inheritance, I believe." The raised inflection made it sound like a question.

"Precisely," he said.

"Only, I wonder, what is your interest in Crystal?" Beth asked.

"I could ask you the same thing. How is it that you became involved in this?" he asked.

Beth briefly recounted the official version of Crystal's disappearance.

As she finished this recitation, Beth heard someone coming up the stairs and the outer office door open then close. She smelled patchouli oil moments before Al appeared in the doorway and glided in. Beth gasped and started to get up.

"Don't be alarmed." Mr. Nobis motioned for her to stay seated. "Mr. Peterson is a client. He is also here at my request."

"Hi there." Al nodded toward Beth and favored her with what, she supposed, was meant to be a seductive smile as he flung his parka across the back of the other chair, revealing a paisley shirt with several of the top buttons undone, showing off his sparse chest hair and gold chains. Then he slumped down in the chair, legs akimbo. "What's happening?" he asked Mr. Nobis.

"Miss Williams was just telling me how she saw Miss Jones topple down the railroad berm in Central Park one night, and then disappear. You wouldn't happen to know anything about that, would you?"

Al stiffened briefly, and narrowed his eyes. "Me? No way. I've been looking for that little chick, too. But she's vanished."

He brought his fingers together and then opened them suddenly. "Like, poof. You know, man."

"So, you have no idea of her whereabouts," Mr. Nobis said.

"No. Why should I? Say what's this all about? What are you laying on me?"

"I'm not 'laying' anything on you. I have an interest in Miss Jones' well-being, and I was hoping you could elucidate her current location."

"Nope. Like I said before, the chick took off, is all. She does that sometimes, and then comes crawling back to me to take what she's got coming." He had dropped his phony smile, scowled, and his face reddened. "Only this time, there's no takesie-backsies. I burned her shit and if I ever see her again, I'll burn her, too."

Beth glared at him in disgust. Al noticed her glare.

"Just kidding, sugar. I'm a lover, not a killer," he said to her.

"Try to remember that," Mr. Nobis said. "I might not be able to keep you out of jail next time. Well, if you do hear from her, please let me know. I'll make it worth your while. That goes for both of you."

"Why's that?" Al eyed him, suspiciously.

"Miss Jones owes me for services rendered and I'd like to get paid. That's all I'm at liberty to say, I'm afraid. Now, if you don't mind, it's been a long day. Please see yourself out." He said to Al.

Al jumped up, grabbed his jacket, and stormed out. Beth started to get up, too.

Mr. Nobis said, "If you have another moment, or two…"

"Okay, but I don't have any information about where Crystal is, now, either."

"No, but I understand you've been doing some investigation."

"You understand? Who have you been talking to?"

"Different people. You know how it is; it's hard to keep secrets in a small town."

"True." Beth paused. "Maybe we can help each other. There is one thing I'd like to know, and maybe you can help with that. Then, we could share some of our discoveries."

"What is it you'd like to know?"

"It seems that Crystal had a post office box. I'd like to know what's in it, but I don't know how I can find out. Could you get a court order, or something, to get into it?"

He linked his hands behind his head, leaned back, and thought for a moment.

"I'll look into it. Let me make a note." He grabbed a leather-bound calendar and a pen. "What is your home number?"

Beth told him, he jotted it down, stood up, and held out his hand.

"If I find out anything, I'll let you know."

Beth got up and shook his hand. "Sounds good. I look forward to hearing from you."

As she clumped down the stairs in her heavy winter boots and stepped back out into the biting cold, she mulled over how she'd handled that. *Pretty good, almost like a character out of a book. It helps to pretend you know what you're doing.*

Chapter 19

The butter was a yellow iceberg after sitting in her car's trunk all afternoon. Beth would have to wait for it to thaw. She dropped a couple of frozen sticks into her one-and-only metal mixing bowl and placed it near the stove. That's okay. She was sure that Evie would be happy to help her mix up the cookie dough. Meanwhile, she turned on the oven and put in a frozen TV dinner.

After changing into jeans, a sweatshirt, and warm wooly socks—a Christmas gift from her mom—she turned on the TV and curled up on the couch with Chestnut to watch the evening news. What a day it had been. She had a lot to tell Evie. The next thing she knew, she was awakened by someone pounding on her front door, which sent Chestnut flying, his claws digging into her thighs as he vaulted off of her. Smoke was pouring out of her kitchen.

She ran to the front door and threw it open. Evie ran past her, followed by a wave of frigid air.

"Are you burning down the house?" she yelled as she rushed toward the kitchen.

"I must have fallen asleep," Beth said.

She closed the door and trailed Evie into the kitchen. She was standing with a blackened TV dinner in one hand, looking around for a place to deposit it.

"I'm pretty sure this is beyond hope," Evie said as she dropped it into the sink and turned on the faucet. "You should get a smoke alarm, or an oven timer, or both." Once it stopped sizzling, she turned off the water and started wrestling with the window over the sink. She managed to open it a crack, and the smoke started to stream out. Coughing, she said, "Let's go into the living room until the smoke clears."

"Go ahead. I'll make a peanut butter sandwich for my supper and join you. Do you want anything?"

"No thanks, I'm good," Evie said and left the kitchen.

When Beth came into the living room, carrying her sandwich on a plate and a glass of milk, Evie had divested herself of most of her wraps. Chestnut was attacking her boot laces as she attempted to take them off.

"Thanks, Evie," Beth said.

"For what?"

"You probably saved my life, again, by showing up when you did." Beth settled into the chair and put her plate and glass on the end table.

"Again? When was the first time?"

"Any of a million times when I was dying of boredom in high school. But I was thinking of the time I fell out of a tree, broke my leg, and you ran for help."

"I remember. We were in fourth grade," Evie laughed. "Well, I didn't have much of a choice. I couldn't carry you."

"You coulda just left me lying there, I suppose. Like that ratfink Clem Daniels, who dared me to climb higher than him, and then ran off when I fell." Beth rubbed at her leg where Chestnut had scratched her while making his escape. "Funny that Chestnut didn't wake me up sooner. He took off like a rocket when you knocked on the door."

"Maybe he doesn't know he's supposed to be a fire alarm cat."

"Hang on," Beth said. She went into the kitchen and poked at the butter sticks, and then returned. "At least the butter is soft, if a bit smoky."

"Butter? What's that for?"

"I was going to surprise you with some home-baked cookies. My mom gave me her recipe and a pan yesterday. And, I went to the grocery store over my lunch break for ingredients." Beth paused for a bite of her sandwich and some milk.

"Oh, this is big news," she continued. "I ran into Mr. Nobis while I was there, and he asked me to come to his office after work."

"Really? What did he want?" Evie asked.

"Information, I guess. He must have found out I was looking for Crystal, and he is also looking for her. I'll tell you all about it later.

"Tell me now."

"Patience, patience...anyway, I left the groceries in my car, and I got home later than usual. So, the butter was frozen solid."

"I appreciate the thought. To think, you skipped lunch on my account. Although, I would have appreciated cookies even more."

Beth laughed. "Oh, don't worry, I didn't skip lunch. Want to help me make the cookies?"

"Sure. But first, tell me what Mr. Nobis said," Evie demanded.

Beth repeated the gist of their conversation. "There was some kind of inheritance for Crystal, I know that much. He let that slip when we were in the grocery store. I told him that I knew she got a letter from him. He must have assumed that I'd seen the contents of the letter, not just the envelope."

"Yeah, that was weird, wasn't it? I wonder where the letter is, and why it got separated from the envelope."

"I don't know. Anyway, I asked him to share information. I said I'll tell him what I know if he tells me what's in Crystal's post office box."

"Can he get into her post office box? Isn't that tampering with the US mail?"

"He said he'd try. Maybe he can get a court order, has power of attorney, or something. Guess who else was there."

"Who?"

"Al. Sleazy Al, the pimp."

"You're kidding."

"Nope. I was there when he arrived, preceded by a wave of patchouli oil and reefer stink."

Evie laughed at the description. Beth didn't mention how terrified she'd been when he appeared, or that he might be stalking her. It was probably all in her head, anyway. There was no reason to frighten Evie.

"Why did Mr. Nobis want both of you there at the same time?"

"That's a good question. I guess he wanted to see our reaction to each other. Or, he wanted to let Al know that he knew I was looking for Crystal. Maybe to warn him off from any kind of retaliation against me. He's Al's lawyer and is trying to keep him out of trouble. Mr. Nobis asked Al if he knew where Crystal was. Al said he didn't know, but he sure got riled up about it. It seemed like he had a real connection to her, and was angry at her for running out on him."

"Angry enough to kill?" Evie asked.

"Maybe. I found out more about their relationship when I phoned Crystal's foster-mom last night."

"So, you got hold of her. What did she have to say?"

"Come on, let's go into the kitchen and get started on those cookies," Beth said and washed down the last bite of her sandwich. "And I'll tell you all about it."

The girls went into the kitchen, closed the window, and turned on the oven. Chestnut took over the warm spot of the couch where Evie had been sitting.

Beth said, "Before I forget, can you come with me to Miss Tanner's house on Saturday morning at 10:00?"

"I think so. Why? What's up?"

"Her antiquities expert is going to be there and he wants to talk to us about the ring."

"Don't you have to be at the library?"

"No, we don't have Saturday or evening hours this week."

"That's right. Okay, I've always wanted to see the inside of her house. She lives in that big, spooky Victorian place out on the edge of town, doesn't she?"

"Yeah, that's the one." Beth grinned. "Remember how we used to dare each other to go there for trick-or-treating when we were kids?"

"Uh-huh, but it was too far to walk and our parents wouldn't drive us out there. This should be fun. Shall I pick you up?"

"No, that would take you out of the way, and you've been doing all the driving, lately. I'll pick you up this time."

They arranged a time.

Beth and Evie stood next to each other in front of the small countertop. Beth measured, while Evie read out the ingredients, and stirred them in.

"First put in the sugar, and I'll cream it in with the butter," Evie said.

"Okay. But, I don't have a measuring cup. Will this work?" Beth held up a thick, brown mug.

"Hang on," Evie said. She examined Beth's assortment of cups and picked out a small china cup embellished with flowers. "This one looks more like the right size. How is it that you don't have any baking equipment?"

"Ernie never ate sweets, so I had no one to bake for except myself, and I was always trying to lose weight, so I never did any baking," Beth said. She scooped up the sugar and dumped it into the bowl. "What's next?"

"Once I get this creamed together, we'll add the eggs, so get those out. You were going to tell me about your conversation with Crystal's foster mother."

"Yeah. She seemed nice. She was very concerned about Crystal and anxious to find out what happened to her. By the way, her first name is Marsha. She said Donna is Crystal's half-sister. She must have been the one who was going to meet Crystal at the train station. I got her phone number from Mrs. Johnson, but I haven't gotten hold of her, yet."

"So Crystal had a half-sister. Same mom?"

"Nope, same dad. But, Crystal never lived with him. She lived with her mom when she could. She wasn't very stable—problems with alcohol and mental health. According to Mrs. Johnson, Crystal wasn't sure who her dad was. Her mom never talked about him. Maybe he was just a one-night stand.

"Anyway, Crystal was in and out of foster care. She'd go to one foster family when her mom was in rehab, and then back to her mom. They moved around a lot, too. Crystal ended up with the Johnson family for her last couple years of high school, after her mom passed away."

"Sounds rough." Evie stopped stirring. "Okay, I'm ready for the eggs now."

Beth cracked them into the mixing bowl. "Yeah, it must have been rough. Mrs. Johnson said Crystal was pretty emotionally closed off by the time she came to live with their family. And, she remembered Al. She said they could see, right away, that he was no good."

"Crystal started dating Al when she was living with the Johnsons?"

"Yeah. Mrs. Johnson said she couldn't convince her that he was trouble. The more she said against him, the more Crystal was determined to sneak out and be with him. She said she wasn't surprised when Crystal finally ran off with him, but she was really surprised that they'd stuck around the area. Like Rosemary told us, he'd promised to take Crystal to California. I didn't have the heart to tell her how Crystal ended up. I just said they lived in the country, outside of town."

"Too bad she fell for Al." Evie paused, thinking about it. Shook her head and then said, "Okay, back to work. It's time to add the salt, baking powder, and vanilla."

"I don't have a measuring spoon. Will a regular teaspoon work?"

"I guess so. I think cookies are pretty forgiving, but get some real measuring cups and spoons before you attempt a cake."

"Yes ma'am. Baking powder—is that the round box, or the square one?"

"The round one. Don't you remember anything from home ec?"

"Oh, I remember plenty. Like the time you used powdered sugar instead of flour by mistake. The cake batter rose like a volcano as it heated up in the oven, flowed out of the pan, and burned all over the bottom of the oven. I'm not the only one to smoke out a room."

They laughed at the memory until tears ran down their cheeks.

"Yeah, I'll never live that down," Evie said when she finally caught her breath. "In my defense, the flour and powdered sugar were in identical containers."

When all the ingredients had been incorporated into the dough, Evie cut off a small chunk of butter and smeared it across the cookie sheet, and then they scooped spoonfuls of dough and plopped them onto the pan.

"Well, you certainly have upped your baking game since high school. I was wondering how I'd manage to grease the pan without a pastry brush. You knew just what to do," Beth said.

"I've done a lot of baking since high school. My brothers inhale sweets. But, the proof of the cookies is in the eating. Pop the pan in." Evie checked the time on the wall clock. "We'll have our proof in 8-10 minutes. Meanwhile, put on the kettle for tea, and finish the story."

"There's not much more to tell. The Johnsons haven't heard from Crystal since she ran off with Al. And they moved to the cities shortly thereafter. She made me promise to let her know when we find Crystal."

Evie grimaced. "If we find her."

"Yeah. We were going to look, remember? But, I don't know where to start. Maybe we'll think of something. How's your Saturday looking? Do you have time to do some investigating after we meet with Miss Tanner's antiquities expert?"

"Yeah, I think so. If I get my chores done tomorrow, so my mom won't fuss at me for taking off."

"If you're sure. I don't want to cause trouble," Beth said.

"Absolutely. Sounds interesting. I'd rather not just sit around home all quarter break."

The teakettle whistled and they stopped to make their tea.

"Time to check the cookies," Evie said, pointing to the clock.

Beth pulled the cookie sheet out of the oven. They had spread out and were flatter than the ones her mom made, but they smelled great and looked done and edible.

"Hey, look, we made cookies," she crowed.

While they nibbled on cookies, Chestnut wandered into the kitchen and rubbed against their legs.

"Pretty good, don't you think?" Beth asked.

"Really good. The smoky note adds a bit of *Je ne sais quoi*," Evie said.

Beth broke off a tiny edge of her cookie and dropped it on the floor. Chestnut sniffed at it, licked it, and then ate it daintily before he retreated to a spot in front of the oven to clean his paws.

Chapter 20

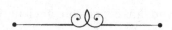

Beth knocked on Miss Tanner's door, and it was opened by a young woman wearing jeans. She glanced at them through long bangs, mumbled something, gestured that they should come in, and then wandered off. Beth and Evie were standing in the hall. They looked at each other and shrugged.

A few moments later, Miss Tanner appeared. She wore a flowing, leopard-print pantsuit and pumps, instead of her usual tweed and heels. However, her hair was in the usual beehive and, as always, her horn-rimmed glasses hung on a beaded chain around her neck.

"Oh, there you are. I'm so glad you could make it," she trilled. "Take off your things, won't you. You can hang up your jackets there." She pointed to the looming wooden hall tree and storage bench, featuring intricate figures of birds and foliage carved into a dark oak frame around a large mirror. "Then, come and join us in the living room, won't you?"

She glided away down the hall, turned right, and disappeared through an open doorway.

They followed her into the next room. There, a short, balding man jumped to his feet and nodded.

"Good morning, ladies," he said.

"Girls, may I introduce Professor Aparduri, a cultural anthropologist and an expert on ancient jewelry. He is a University of Minnesota professor of anthropology, a certified gemologist, and, I may add, my cousin."

"The most illustrious of all my credentials, I'm sure," he interjected.

Miss Tanner gave him a tight smile, seeming a bit irritated at the interruption. "As I was saying, Professor Aparduri, may I present Miss Beth Williams and Miss Evie Hanson."

"Charmed, I'm sure," he said and nodded.

"Please, call me Beth."

"And, call me Evie."

"Of course, pleased to meet both of you," he nodded again.

He reminded Beth of one of those little novelty bird toys that you see on windowsills, with a glass of water in front of them. You start them bobbing, they dip their beaks into the water and keep on bobbing.

"Wonderful," Miss Tanner said. "Now that we all know one another, take a seat. I'm going to see if Madeline needs a hand bringing in the coffee."

She glided out of the room, trailing a woodsy scent in her wake.

Beth and Evie glanced at each other. Beth shrugged, almost imperceptibly, and then they took a seat next to each other on the striped, straight-backed loveseat. The professor sat back down, across the coffee table from them, on a matching chair.

The professor fidgeted and harrumphed a bit, and then said, "Olivia tells me that you girls found this ring." He fished it out of a pocket in his tweed jacket, held it up at eye level, and examined it. "A very interesting object. How did you happen to find it?"

"Well, we found it...?" Beth hesitated and looked at Evie.

"On Sunday, the day after you found the body," Evie said.

"That's right. I found what I assumed was a body on Saturday evening, December 21st." Beth repeated the story.

Professor Aparduri listened intently, nodding from time to time.

"And, the police wouldn't investigate," Beth concluded. "So, Evie and I went to take a look around the next afternoon, and that's when we found it."

"Ah, yes. Very unusual, I'm sure. Well, what I can tell you about it..." He stopped mid-sentence as Miss Tanner paraded back into the room, and he pocketed the ring.

She carried a coffee pot in one hand and a tray of pastries in the other. Madeline trailed behind her, carrying a larger tray of crockery, spoons, napkins, a cream pitcher, and a sugar bowl. They placed these items on a sideboard.

"Thank you, Madeline. You may return to your other tasks," Miss Tanner said.

Madeline mumbled something, and then turned and left the room.

"Madeline is a neighbor girl I employ to help me out with cleaning and the occasional other tasks. She's still learning," Miss Tanner said. Then, she invited her guests to have some refreshments.

After everyone had helped themselves and resumed their seats, she said, "I hope I didn't interrupt you, Gerald."

"Not at all." He patted with a napkin at the flake of frosting that clung to the edge of his mouth. "Beth had just finished telling me how she and Evie found the ring, and I was about to tell them what little I can about it. The abraxas stone, or abrasax, as it is sometimes known, appears to be genuine and may date back to the second century."

"Wow!" Beth and Evie said, in unison.

"Is it valuable?" Beth asked

"An interesting question. While this stone may be quite ancient, it may not be particularly rare. Hence, not especially valuable."

He paused for a sip of coffee and another bite of his pastry.

"You see, a great many of these types of stones were created. As far as we can ascertain, they were used as a type of good luck charm."

"I read something about it. It had to do with the Basilidian Gnostics," Beth said.

"Yes, that is quite true. Basilides of Egypt was a second-century Gnostic teacher, and he considered Abraxas a god who ruled the 365 circles of creation. One for each day of the year. The numerical value of the Greek letters that make up the word abraxas is 365."

"Why would a Greek word be inscribed on an Egyptian object?" Beth asked.

"My, you do ask interesting questions, Beth." He turned to Miss Tanner. "You certainly have a bright young assistant."

Miss Tanner simply smiled and inclined her head.

"Scholars differ on the matter. But, it is known that the Greek alphabet was widely used in ancient times, and spread along with the spread of Christianity. Gnosticism is an offshoot of Christianity, and Basilidians are a type of Gnostics."

Evie wiped crumbs from her fingers and put down her plate and napkin, and asked, "What is Gnosticism?"

"Ah, also an excellent question. Gnosticism is not one thing, but a group of cults that originated in the first century AD. Details vary from sect to sect, but they all believe in the power of gnosis, which is the Greek word for knowledge, from firsthand, mystical experience. Which they believe they have. They are a blend of Christianity with elements from other older religious ideas and practices, such as the Babylonian, Egyptian, and Eleusinian mysteries. In the second century, the early church fathers labeled them as heresies and destroyed many of their texts, making it difficult for scholars, today."

"That is all very fascinating, I'm sure, Gerald," Miss Tanner said. "But tell the girls what you told me about the ring."

"The ring? Oh, yes." He turned from his runaway train of thought, and pulled the ring out of his pocket, held it up at eye level, paused, and pronounced, "Although the stone is ancient, the rest of the ring is not."

He sat back and enjoyed their astonishment as the girls exclaimed, looked at each other, then at Miss Tanner, and then back at the professor.

"Oh, yes. I believe one often finds these stones repurposed to create contemporary jewelry. In this case, some effort was made to artificially age the metal, but the wear patterns and the methods for mounting made it immediately apparent to me, as it would be to any other gemologist, that it is a recent creation."

"So, that means, what, that the ring is not very valuable?" Beth asked.

"No, I wouldn't say that. It is genuine in the sense of being made from precious metals.

"Silver, correct," Evie said.

"No, not silver. It's 14-carat white gold. And it is quite hefty, as you'd expect from a man's ring. I estimate that it might be worth around $800 to $1,000."

"Really? As much as that?" Evie said. "In that case, I think we'd better turn it over to the police. Someone will be looking for it."

The others agreed.

Beth and Evie decided their first stop after Miss Tanner's house should be the police station. They parked in the parking lot in front of the nondescript brick building, next to the courthouse. Beth's mouth felt dry as she approached the building. She eyed the barred windows of the jail cells that were located on the second floor and wondered who was up there. She glanced around, hoping no one else was watching them. She'd never been inside the police station before, and approaching it made her feel a bit nervous and guilty.

Beth hung back as Evie looked at her quizzically, and then preceded her through the door. They approached the desk sergeant, sitting with his back to them and talking to someone behind him.

He swiveled around in his chair and said, "Hello there, ladies. Can I help you with something?"

"Is Officer Crample here?" Evie asked.

"Yup, I think I saw him around here, somewhere."

"Can we talk to him?"

"Sure, I guess so. Hold on and I'll get him." He rose and hitched his pants up to the bottom of his beer belly. "Watch the desk, for me, okay?" he said to the person hidden behind a room divider.

"Sure thing," a male voice answered. But, no one appeared.

Beth and Evie looked at each other, smiled nervously, and Evie shrugged. A few minutes elapsed before the desk sergeant reappeared, followed by Bill Crample.

"Hello, there. I wasn't expecting you two. To what do I owe the pleasure?" he asked.

Beth said, "We're here about the case."

"Come on back with me," he said with a smirk.

Beth and Evie trailed him through a door into the next room. The overhead fluorescent lights, and the dim daylight that struggled through two smudged windows, did nothing to enhance the bleak, rectangular room. The walls were painted an unattractive shade of green and the floor covering was a worn, gray tile. Six metal desks, littered with folders, phones, typewriters, and assorted paraphernalia, each desk with an adjacent metal filing cabinet, formed two rows along the outer walls. One of the desks, in the back, was occupied by a cop who glanced up with a disinterested expression, then returned to typing something on a battered manual typewriter, using only two fingers, pausing to unstick keys and mutter curses.

Crample took a seat behind one of the middle desks. He grunted something that Evie took to mean "have a seat," and then watched, mutely, as they sat on the two battered metal chairs in front of his desk, removed their hats and gloves, loosened their scarves, and unzipped their jackets.

Once they were settled, he said, "So, what can I do for you?"

"It's about the ring," Beth started.

He sighed, audibly.

"Yes, well, you may not want to know this." She paused as she dug through her purse, wishing she wasn't there, and then pulled out the ring. "But we've just been told, by an expert, that this is a valuable object."

She related their meeting with Dr. Aparduri, and what he'd told them about the ring.

"So, you see, it is a valuable item that someone lost, and they will certainly contact the police, at some point, to reclaim it."

"I suppose so." He reluctantly admitted. "But, they haven't come forward, as of yet."

"Which might cause one to wonder why. Don't you think?" Beth said.

He looked at her with exasperation. "Okay, maybe. Well, hand it over. I guess I'll do a report and put it in lost and found. Is that all?"

"Will you let us know if anyone reclaims it?" Evie asked. "After all, if no one does, it's ours. Finders keepers, right?"

"Yup, I'll let you know. Anything else?"

"Are we keeping you from something?" Beth asked.

"Just from doing my job. I'm supposed to be heading out on patrol."

"In that case, we won't take up any more of your time." Beth stood, abruptly, and her chair slid back and banged against the desk behind her. She'd intended to tell him about her conversations with Crystal's foster mother, Al, and Mr. Nobis. Clearly, he still didn't take the whole thing seriously and was eager to get rid of them. She turned and walked away.

Evie said to Crample, "Thanks for your time. We'll be in touch." She hurried to catch up with Beth, who stood, hand on the door to the outer office, waiting for her.

After they'd left the building and got back into her car, Beth said, "He's so maddening. It was like he could not care less about anything."

"I know. Well, at least we got rid of that ring," Evie said.

"True. Once I found out how much it was worth, I just didn't want to be responsible for it any longer. Plus, it was kind of creepy, wasn't it?"

"Yeah, it was. Well, it's Bill Crample's problem, now. Where to next?" Evie said.

"Have you talked to Sam about dating Beverly, yet?"

"Nope. I tried a couple of times, but he wasn't around when I stopped by. He was scheduled to be at work, but didn't' show."

"From what I've heard, that's not too unusual. He's not the most reliable guy. Okay, how about we stop at the garage. Maybe Sam is there now."

Chapter 21

Beth followed Evie into Gary's auto repair shop. The bell rang as they entered, and they were enveloped in the familiar odors of oil and exhaust that clung to her brother's clothes. No one was sitting at the reception desk. Gary poked his head around the corner into the office area, holding a wrench in one hand.

"Hi, Beth. Hi Evie. I'll be right with you," he said.

"I guess Sam isn't working, today," Beth said to Evie.

After a bit of clanking in the next room, Gary came in, wiping his hands on an oily rag. "Problems with your car, Beth?"

"No, it's running great. Thanks again for working on it. We're looking for Sam. Is he working today?" Beth said.

"Supposed to be." Gary frowned. "He didn't show—again."

"Again?" Evie asked.

"Yeah, I haven't seen him since Thursday. I'd fire him, but he works cheap, and I can't pay more for more reliable help. And, he does know a lot about cars."

"Have you called to check up on him?" Evie asked.

"Naw. He'll get in touch when he sobers up. That's usually what happens. Why? Was there something special you wanted to talk to him about?"

Evie looked at Beth, and Beth said, "We're trying to set him up with Beverly. You know, the teller at the First National Bank."

"You're kidding. Why?"

"She has a crush on him, and she said she'll give me information about Crystal if we can get Sam to ask her out."

After Gary stopped laughing, Beth told him the whole story.

"Wow, that's rich. Sam and Beverly. I'd never have put those two together. I guess you never know. Okay, I'll give him a call, and see what's what," he said.

He sat behind the desk and pulled the green phone, covered in oil smudges, toward him and dialed.

"Hello, Mrs. Daniels, this is Gary Williams, from the garage. Is Sam there?" He paused, listening. "Not since Thursday? Have you contacted anyone about it?" Another pause. "I see. Well, thank you." He looked up at Beth and Evie and shrugged. "Okay, let me know if you do, and I'll call you if I see him first." He hung up.

"Was that his mother? It sounds like she hasn't seen him, either," Beth said.

"Yeah, not since Thursday. That's weird. I wonder where he is. But she didn't seem too concerned. She said he comes and goes and it's not unusual for him to be gone for a few days, especially if he's seeing someone. She didn't say as much, but it sounds like he'll shack up with a girl until he needs a change of clothes, or she kicks him out."

"Did Sam say anything about a new girl he's seeing or anything else that might give us a clue?"

"No, nothing like that." He paused, leaned back in the swivel chair, and stared up at the worn acoustic tiles on the ceiling. "The last thing we talked about was that car you followed from the Big Boy."

"You mean the black Pontiac?" Evie said.

"Yeah. Remember how I said that Mr. Gloor couldn't have been driving it, because it was here that weekend. I asked Sam if Mr. Gloor had come back for it that evening before he closed up for the night or something."

"Had he?" Beth asked.

"He said no. Come to think of it, he acted kind of weird about it. He wanted to know why I was asking. I told him about Crystal and that you were looking for her, and then he got all kind of quiet." Gary picked up a pencil and tapped the eraser end on the desk.

"Gary," Beth said. "I told you not to tell anyone about me finding her."

"No, you said to stick with the official version that you saw her roll down the hill, she was stunned by the fall, recovered, and now she's missing. That's what I told him. Anyway, I think everyone in town knows you thought she was dead. You said so in front of a bunch of people, including Sam's little brother."

"Oh, right. So, I wonder why he acted weird when you talked to him about it."

"Good question." Gary leaned back in his chair and studied the ceiling, again. "You know, now that I think about it, Sam might have been driving that car."

"What?" Evie and Beth both exclaimed.

"That would make sense. You said you never saw the driver, right?" Gary said.

"That's right," Beth said.

"And, he was driving fast in the general direction of this shop. Right?" Gary said.

"True," Beth said.

"It all makes sense," Gary said. "That's why he acted weird when I asked him about the car. If he took it out for a spin and used it to pick up a girl, when I asked him about it and said you were looking for Crystal, he may have thought I was implying he had something to do with her disappearance."

"Maybe he did," Evie said.

Beth and Gary both looked at her, mouths open.

"No way," Gary said. "Sam has his faults, but he's no killer."

"What if he was drunk and he got too physical with her," Beth said. "It might have been an accident. You used to date him, Evie; did he ever get rough with you?"

"No," Evie said. "He was always sweet to me. Just, too interested in other girls. But, that was years ago. We were kids. Maybe he's changed for the worse."

"I kind of doubt he's changed that much," Gary said as he stood up. "Well, I'd better get back to work. As you know, I'm short-handed, today. I'll let you know if Sam turns up."

"Where to next?" Evie asked as they walked out to Beth's car.

"I think we should go back out to Al's place and try to talk to Sarah or Dawn, again. Maybe Sam went out there."

They got in, and Beth started the car.

"Why would he do that?" Evie asked.

"If he was driving the black Pontiac that we followed from the Big Boy, could be that wasn't the first time he picked up one of Al's girls. Maybe one of those girls was Crystal."

"So, Sam might have known her," Evie said.

"Sounds like it," Beth said. "When Gary asked him about the car and talked about Crystal's disappearance, he might have decided to go see Al."

"That's a stretch. Why would he do that? He already knew about Crystal's disappearance. As Gary said, his little brother must have told him about it when it happened."

"You're right. Maybe he didn't. But, if he suddenly realized that Al might know what happened to Crystal, and if he liked her, he might have decided to confront Al about it. Want to go out there and find out?"

"I don't know. What if Al is there?"

"What if he is? He doesn't scare me," Beth said, trying to sound braver than she was. She remembered how she'd crept around her apartment, locking doors and checking windows, after she thought she saw Al's car driving down her alley. "Anyway, we'll only stop if we don't see his car parked out front."

"Doesn't scare you, huh, fearless leader?" Evie said.

They both laughed.

"Okay, I guess it's worth a try," Evie said.

Beth put the car in gear and drove off. They hadn't gone too far down Main Street before a patrol car pulled up behind them, and turned on his flashers and siren.

"What the heck? I wasn't going too fast, was I?" Beth said as she glanced at the speedometer. She pulled over, stopped, and watched in the rearview mirror as Bill Crample got out of the squad car and approached them. "Oh, no," she said, and then swore under her breath.

She rolled down her window, and he leaned in.

"What's the problem, officer? Was I going too fast?" Beth asked.

"Nope. Hi Beth. Hi Evie. I wanted to give you girls a heads up, in case you're planning on heading out of town. The weather report says there's a storm heading this way."

"No kidding? That's why you pulled me over?" Beth said. It seemed kind of suspicious that he would pull over motorists to warn them about a weather report. Or, was this just an excuse to harass her? "When is this storm supposed to hit us?"

"Not until after dark. But, if I were you, I'd stay off the open highway, just in case."

She felt like telling him where he could stuff his warning, but put on a sweet smile, instead.

"Thanks for the warning. We'll keep that in mind. By the way, I was just talking to my brother, and it seems that Sam Daniels has gone missing."

"Another missing person? You seem to trip over them." He laughed at his little joke. "When did he go missing? It must have been pretty recent."

"Thursday. That's the last time my brother or Sam's mom saw him."

"Well, then, he's not missing. I saw him this morning."

"When was this? Where?"

"A couple of hours ago. He was headed north." He pointed in the direction Beth and Evie had been going. "Probably heading to Grand Bend, if I was guessing. Going too fast, as usual. That's why I noticed him"

"Did you give him a ticket?"

"Naw, not worth it. He already has a bunch of them, and never pays. Anyway, he slowed down when he noticed me."

Beth snapped. "Well, it's been really nice talking to you. If there's nothing else, we should get going." She started to roll up the window.

"Ladies." He stepped back, nodded as he touched his cap, and returned to his squad car.

"What a jerk," Beth said

"I guess so," Evie said. "So, Sam is alive and well. Just goofing off, as usual." She paused, and then said, "Do you think Bill is right about the storm?"

"Could be. But, when isn't there a chance? Winter storms are possible from October to May. A person can't stay in all winter. Besides, he said it wasn't coming until dark, and we'll be back before then." She turned on the radio. "We'll listen to the weather report, just in case."

Chapter 22

Beth took the highway out of town and then followed it as it turned west, toward Grand Bend. The snow blew across the road, wraith-like, swirling into ever-changing patterns, as her car radio blasted out the top-ten hits, and the heater hummed along. Beth noticed a familiar vehicle approaching, driving fast.

"Isn't that Sam's truck?" she said.

Evie leaned forward, and they both watched it fly past. Sam was hunkered down behind the steering wheel, scowling, his eyes staring straight ahead. He didn't respond when Beth raised a hand in greeting.

"Yup, that was him," Evie said.

"So, he's definitely not missing. He sure didn't look happy, though. Did he?"

"Nope. I wonder where he came from."

As they approached the turn onto the gravel road to Al's place, Beth noticed a dark plume of smoke rising into the leaden gray sky.

"Look." Beth pointed toward it. "Do you think that's coming from Al's place?"

"It could be," Evie said.

Beth sped up. As they drew near, it became clear that was, indeed, the source of the smoke. She turned into the driveway and when they cleared the windbreak, she saw smoke pouring out of the windows of the house. Sarah, wearing a miniskirt, slippers, and an oversized, beige sweater, knelt on the snow-covered roof of the porch and held out a hand to Dawn who, wearing pajamas, her hair in curlers, was crawling out of a window. Beth parked the car. She and Evie jumped out and ran toward the house.

Dawn and Sarah tiptoed, and slid toward the edge of the porch, stopped, and looked down, hesitating.

"Sit down, and then jump!" Beth shouted out.

They still hesitated. Looking from Beth and Evie to the ground, below.

"I'm scared," Sarah said.

"It's okay," Evie called out. "Come on. Jump into the snow. You won't get hurt."

After further encouragement, they sat on the edge of the roof, pushed off with their hands, and landed into the snowbank at the base of the house. They jumped up, sputtering, covered with snow, but unhurt. Sarah fished around in the snow and retrieved her slippers. Dawn had only socks on her feet.

"Come on. Let's get into the car," Beth said. She ran over and opened the back door and held it open. Coughing and shivering, Sarah and Dawn climbed in. Beth got the blanket, which her dad had insisted she carry with her in the winter, out of the car's trunk and handed it to the girls.

"Where's Al? Is he still in the house?" Beth asked.

"I don't know," Sarah said. Her mascara had started to streak down her cheeks, giving her the appearance of a sad clown. "There was a fight, and then everything went quiet. I don't know if he is still in the house or not."

"A fight with you?" Beth asked.

"No, with a man who came to the house," Sarah said.

Evie was standing behind Beth. She said to her, "Let's get into the car. It's freezing out here."

They got in, and Beth started the car.

"So you don't know if Al is still in the house, or not," Beth said.

Beth and Evie shifted sideways to look at the girls sitting in the back seat. Sarah and Dawn, their faces smudged with soot, both shook their heads, wordlessly. They seemed to be in shock. They shivered and huddled together under the blanket. Beth turned the car heater up to high.

"Do you think we should look for him?" Evie asked Beth.

Beth looked at the house. Smoke was pouring out of the open upstairs window.

"No, it's too risky. We should wait for the firemen," Beth said. "Did you call them?" Beth asked the girls in the back seat.

"Yeah, I called," Dawn said.

"How long ago?" Beth asked.

"Just before we climbed out the window. There was too much smoke to go downstairs." She coughed. "So, I used the upstairs phone in Al's bedroom. He wasn't in there, that's all I know for sure. I called down the stairs for him, but he didn't answer."

A wail of sirens headed in their direction and, moments later, a fire truck sped up the driveway. Firemen jumped out and started hooking up hoses to the truck's water tank. One of them ran over to the car. Beth rolled down her window.

"Are you girls okay?" he asked.

"Yeah, we're okay," Beth said.

"Were you in the house?"

"No, but they were." Beth pointed to the girls in the back seat. "They were climbing out of the upstairs window when we got here."

The fireman turned his attention to the girls in the back seat.

"Is there anyone else in the house?"

"Al might be," Dawn said. "We don't know if he left the house or not. We were upstairs when the fire started downstairs."

"Al? Is that a child or a man?"

"A man," Dawn said.

"Okay. Sit tight. We'll take a look." He ran back to rejoin the rest of the crew.

A couple of firemen put on long, orange gloves, what looked like gas masks, and strapped air tanks to their backs. They picked up axes and flashlights and headed to the house. When they opened the front door, black smoke poured out and they disappeared into it. Beth and the other girls in the car watched wordlessly, their eyes glued to the entrance as flames started to lick out, along with the smoke.

Time crawled until the firemen reappeared carrying Al's limp body. His arms flopped at his sides as they rushed him away from the burning house, and then placed him on the stretcher that had been set up next to the fire truck. Another fireman covered him with blankets and placed an oxygen mask on his face.

"I guess he's alive," Beth said.

"Should we go to him?" Sarah asked Dawn, her hand on the door handle.

"No, stay here. We'd only get in the way. Besides, we're not dressed for the weather," Dawn said.

More sirens headed in their direction and another fire engine and an ambulance turned into the driveway. The fire truck parked alongside Beth's car, and the ambulance parked behind her, blocking them in.

"It looks like we'll have to stick around for a while," Evie said.

"Yeah, it looks like it." Beth turned toward Sarah and Dawn. "So, Sarah, you said there was a fight. A man came and fought with Al. Did you see him?"

"Yeah, but I don't know who he was. I just glimpsed him and then went back upstairs."

"How about you, Dawn, did you recognize him?"

"I was upstairs the whole time. I didn't see him," Dawn said.

This isn't going anywhere, Beth thought. *Either they don't know who it was, or they don't want to say.* She lapsed into silence and watched as the firemen battled the flames and the ambulance crew went over to Al and helped him sit up. Apparently, he was feeling better.

"I thought I recognized the voice, though," Dawn said.

"You did?" Beth said. She and Evie turned, eagerly, toward Dawn.

"Yeah, I think so. He was a date, you know. He said his name was Sam."

"A date? Did he pick you up at the Big Boy restaurant?" Beth asked.

"Yeah. I was surprised to see him driving that car. When I saw it, I expected someone else."

"What car was it?" Evie asked.

"A big black one," Dawn said.

"Like a Pontiac?" Evie asked.

"Yeah, it could have been," Dawn said.

"When was this?" Beth asked.

"Last weekend," Dawn said.

"That fits," Beth said to Evie. "I guess Sam was driving the car."

"What are you talking about? Who's this Sam?" Sarah asked.

"He's just a guy we know," Beth said. "Actually, we thought we saw him driving the opposite way, on our way out here, but weren't sure it was him. Did you hear what they were fighting about?"

"Not at first, but then it got louder. They were arguing about Crystal," Dawn said.

"Something about 'did Al know where she was' and stuff like that, wasn't it?" Sarah asked Dawn.

"Yeah," Dawn said. "Al must have said he didn't know because Sam started shouting that he didn't believe him."

"And then Al screamed something about throwing Crystal out like the trash she was. Then Sam started cursing at Al, and stuff started crashing around, they must have been fighting. Right Dawn?" Sarah said.

"Yeah, but Al was always saying stuff like that. He didn't mean anything," Dawn said.

Sarah looked at the house and gasped in horror.

"All my stuff is burning up." She started to cry.

"Don't worry about it. We'll stick together and get by," Dawn said.

"The letter is gone, too," Sarah said.

"What letter is that?" Beth asked.

"The one from the lawyer that I found, hidden in Crystal's room. Dawn said maybe we could use it to make Crystal give us some of the money. So, I took it, but I left the envelope so maybe she wouldn't know. And she didn't, neither. She never said nothing about it. Stupid Crystal, always sneaking around. We knew what she was up to. Didn't we, Dawn," Sarah said, between sniffles.

"You talk too much," Dawn said.

"What's the difference? The letter is burned up and Crystal is gone, so it doesn't matter, now," Sarah said.

Sarah fell silent and started whimpering. They all sat in silence, except for Sarah's soft sobbing and Dawn's cursing under her breath, as they watched the house burn and the firemen working to put out the fire.

Another siren sounded, and a Grand Bend police car pulled into the driveway and parked behind them. The police took brief statements from Beth and Evie, and then took Sarah and Dawn away for further questioning.

After Sarah and Dawn left, as Beth and Evie sat in the car watching and waiting. Two EMTs, one on each side of Al, helped him to the ambulance. Soot-streaked and shaky, a blanket draped across his shoulders, he walked past without noticing them. The EMTs loaded him into the back of the ambulance and backed away down the driveway.

The fire trucks started to wrap up their hoses and put away their gear.

"It looks like we can get out of here, now," Beth said.

She drove around the fire trucks, turned, drove past the burned-out house, now a charred wreck adorned with icicles, down the driveway, and out to the road. Once beyond the pine tree windbreak, they emerged into a swirling sea of white.

"The weather has gotten worse," Evie said.

"Yeah, looks like it," Beth said.

Beth slowed to a crawl, feeling her way along, listening for the sound of gravel churning under her tires to keep her on the road, while watching for glimpses of it when the wind dropped or shifted. She could see only a few feet in front of her.

"Do you think we should keep going, or stop and wait it out?" Beth glanced at the speedometer. She was going ten miles an hour. "At this rate, it will take us hours to get back to town, and I don't dare go any faster."

"Let's wait it out," Evie said. "This is too dangerous. Stop at that farmhouse up the road. If they're home, maybe they'll let us call home so they know we're okay, and wait inside. If they're not home, at least we can hang out in their driveway."

"What if they ask us where we're coming from? They'll never believe we just happened to be passing. Where would we be coming from that would lead us down this gravel road?" Beth said.

"I guess we'll just have to tell the truth," Evie said. "We smell like smoked bacon, and they surely will have noticed the fire down the road, so there's no point pretending."

"Yeah, when all else fails…" Beth trailed off.

She slowed even more. Squinting, she searched for the driveway. The sideways-blowing snow made it almost impossible to see beyond the windshield. Finally, she caught a glimpse of lights and the vague outline of the house. She turned in and parked in front of the house.

They got out of the car and dashed to the front door. The temperature had dropped since last they'd been out of the car, and the thirty-below temperature felt like a slap in the face. Beth burrowed her face into her scarf as she banged on the door.

An elderly woman opened the door and motioned them in. "Come in, come in; let's get you out of the cold."

They stepped into the enclosed front porch.

"Leave your boots and coats out here and then come on in," she said. She indicated hooks where they could hang their things.

The farmer's wife went back inside, leaving the door cracked open for them. Beth stepped into the kitchen, filled with the heady aroma of percolating coffee and freshly baked bread. Two bread loaves and a pan of rolls sat on cooling racks on the kitchen counter, next to a bubbling, electric percolator. The farmer, wearing coveralls, sat at a round, wooden table in the middle of the room, reading a newspaper, as his rosy-cheeked wife scurried around setting out dishes and silverware. It looked like they had arrived just in time for a coffee break.

"Wow, it smells great in here," Evie said.

Beth agreed. Her mouth watered, and she realized that they'd missed lunch. Beth and Evie introduced themselves.

"Pleased to meet you," the farmer said. "I'm Fred Olson, and this is my wife, Elsie. From the smoky smell, I guess you girls came from next door. What's going on over there?"

"The house caught fire. It was burning when we got there. We got boxed in by the emergency vehicles, so we had to stay. Meanwhile, the weather got worse," Beth said.

"Oh my," Mr. Olson said, folding his newspaper and laying it on the table. "Was anyone hurt?"

"Everyone got out. Allen had to be carried out of the house by the firemen, but I think he's going to be okay. He was able to walk to the ambulance."

Beth noticed that Mr. and Mrs. Olson exchanged a look of disgust when she mentioned Allen.

"Sarah and Dawn got out of the house before he did. They climbed out of an upstairs window, onto the porch roof, then jumped into the snow. Then, they sat in our car until the police came and took them away."

"Two girls left with the police, you say? What about the other girl? What was her name?" Mr. Olson asked his wife.

"Crystal," Mrs. Olson said. "Yes, what about Crystal? Is she okay?"

Beth was surprised to hear Crystal's name. She looked toward Evie who raised her eyebrows in response.

"She wasn't there. She doesn't live there anymore. So, I gather that you know Crystal," Beth said.

"We met her," Mrs. Olson said. "How do you girls know her?"

"We'll tell you all about it, but we probably should call home first, and let our families know we're okay," Beth said.

Mr. and Mrs. Olson agreed. "And, tell them you'll stay here until the storm passes—most likely tomorrow morning," Mrs. Olson said.

She looked toward her husband, who nodded in agreement. She insisted they should stay, ignoring their protestations that they didn't want to put the Olsons to any extra trouble, and showed them to the phone in the living room. Beth and Evie took turns making their phone calls.

Beth's father said he'd send Gary out, early the next morning, to make sure she could start her car.

"That old thing doesn't always start, real good. That's one reason your grandmother got rid of it. I don't want you girls to get stranded out there," he said.

Beth thought it was likely that Mr. Olson could help her start her car if needed. But, she didn't want to further impose on these nice elderly people that she'd just met, so she readily agreed.

Afterward, Mrs. Olson invited them to join them for coffee and rolls. For the sake of politeness, they half-heartedly refused, but then let themselves be convinced and joined Mr. Olson at the table.

Mrs. Olson buzzed around the kitchen making sure everyone was served before she sat down to join them.

"So, you were saying how you happen to know Allen and the others. If you don't mind my saying so, you don't seem like the type of girls we usually see around there," she said once they were all settled.

Mr. Olson paused, coffee cup in midair, clearly also curious.

Beth, who had just taken a big bite of her cinnamon roll, held up a hand signaling she couldn't talk right now.

Evie said, "We're friends of Crystal's family. She's missing, and we're trying to help them find her. Crystal was last seen before Christmas. Her last known address was out here, living with Allen, Sarah, and Dawn. We wanted to talk to the girls. We thought Crystal might have confided in them and they might know where she went."

Beth was impressed by Evie's quick thinking and the reasonableness of the explanation. Which had the added benefit of being close to the truth. They were friends of Crystal's family—sort of—having met her foster sister, and she'd spoken to her foster mom on the phone.

"I see," Mrs. Olson said. "Friends of her family. But, from what she said, she didn't have a family."

"Well, it's her foster family. Crystal left them and ran away with Allen because they didn't approve of him. And, they haven't seen her since," Beth said.

Again, Beth noticed a look pass between Mr. and Mrs. Olson at the mention of Allen's name.

"They are actually very nice. They hoped Crystal would change her mind and come back home. So, you knew Crystal?" Beth asked.

"As I said, we only met her once, briefly," Mrs. Olson said.

Mr. Olson had silently followed the conversation, and then, suddenly, exclaimed, "That Allen is no good. Too bad he didn't burn up along with the house."

"Now, now, Dad. Don't get worked up." Mrs. Olson patted his hand.

"He's upset because Crystal reminded us of our daughter when she was a girl," Mrs. Olson told Beth and Evie. "She walked over here, one day this past fall, before the snow. She was crying. She had bruises on her face and a swollen lip. He beat her up, you see."

Mr. Olson's face darkened and he mumbled imprecations under his breath.

"Well, let's not talk about that, now," Mrs. Olson said. "Why don't you girls come upstairs with me and help me make up the beds in the spare room."

While they were upstairs with Mrs. Olson, Beth asked her, "What happened next? Did Crystal walk back home or did Allen come and get her?"

"No, she called someone, and they drove out here and picked her up. I was busy canning, so I didn't see who it was. But, later I saw the phone bill, so I know who she called."

"Who was it?" Evie asked.

"I don't know who she spoke to, but she called the rectory at Our Lady of Sorrows Church in Davison City," Mrs. Olson said.

Chapter 23

Weighed down by the heavy patchwork quilt, Beth struggled to free an arm, reached over, and picked the alarm clock up off of the bedside table, which sat between the matching twin beds in the Olson's spare bedroom.

"What time do you think I should set it for?" Beth said. "We don't want to interfere with the morning routine."

"I don't know. How about 7:00?" Evie said, and then yawned.

Beth agreed. She wound the clock, set the alarm, placed it back on the table, and switched off the table lamp before snuggling back under the covers.

"What did you make of what Mrs. Olson said about Crystal?" Beth said.

"You mean how she came over after a fight with Al and called the rectory for a ride?"

"Yeah, that, and the timing of her visit. What do you suppose led up to the fight with Al?"

Evie thrashed around as she turned over in her bed. By the light from the moon and the yard light, streaming in through the gauzy curtained window into the bedroom, Beth saw that Evie was now propped up on her pillow, facing her.

"Man, this quilt weighs a ton," Evie said. "I have a down comforter at home. I don't like heavy blankets." She pushed it down to her waist. "That's better."

"Really? I don't mind. It's like having Chestnut laying on top of me. Except without the purring. I bet he misses me. I hope he's okay," Beth said.

"I'm sure he's okay," Evie said. "He probably loves having the place to himself. He won't miss you until you're late with his breakfast tomorrow morning. So what was it you were saying about Crystal?"

"I was wondering what caused the fight. From what Dawn and Sarah said, Crystal and Al were living together, just the two of them, before they moved in. That could have precipitated a jealous quarrel. It seems like Allen was her boyfriend when she ran off with him. And then, at some point, he became her pimp."

"That's true." Evie paused to pummel her pillow. "We should ask Mrs. Olson in the morning. I bet she knows who came, and when. I don't think she misses much."

"Sounds good." Beth yawned. "I'm pooped. If you're done beating up on your bed, let's try to get some sleep." She rolled over and fell sound asleep.

In what seemed like only a moment, Beth was awakened by voices, the opening and closing of doors, and then the sound of a motor running outside. She sleepily wondered why her parents were up so early. Cozy, under the heavy quilt, she dreamily listened to the morning getting underway around her. It took a while to realize where she was, and who was snoring in the bed next to hers. They were in the Olson's spare bedroom. She glanced at the alarm clock—6:25. The day began early here.

She jumped out of bed, ran across the cold linoleum, and peeked out of the window. The sun wasn't up yet, though the eastern edge of the sky was orange. The yard light was still on. Everything was covered by thick mounds of white snow. It looked like Mr. Olson had already started clearing it. Footsteps in the snow led to the barn, next to a plowed path. A pickup truck, with a snowplow attached to the front of it, was roaring up and down the driveway. Downstairs, Mrs. Olson clattered around in the kitchen, and Beth smelled coffee brewing.

Evie rolled over, and sleepily asked, "What time is it?"

Beth said, "It's about 6:30." She went over and turned off the clock. "I guess we don't need that. Mr. and Mrs. Olson are already up. He's outside, plowing, and I heard Mrs. Olson downstairs in the kitchen. I guess we should get up, too."

As they went downstairs a short time later, Beth heard people stamping snow off of their boots, and men's voices, coming from the front porch. The door opened, letting in a gust of cold air, and Beth's brother, Gary, and Mr. Olson came inside. Their cheeks bright red from the cold.

"Hi Gary," Beth said. "You're early."

"Hi, Sis. Yeah, I've been up most of the night. Me and Sam have been taking turns driving the tow truck and sitting by the phone in the office. I only got a few catnaps between calls. The storm hit kind of fast yesterday. There are cars in the ditches, all up and down the highway."

"So Sam made it back okay?"

"Yup, I guess he was just out for a couple of days like I thought." Gary blew on his red hands, and clapped them together to warm them. "I tried to start your car, Beth. But, it's a no-go. I'll have to tow it back to town. Anyway, you'd never make it out to the highway. The road from here to there hasn't been plowed, yet. If you're ready, let's get going. I need to get back to work."

"Can't you at least stop for a cup of coffee?" Mrs. Olson asked.

Gary let himself be persuaded to stay for a quick cup of coffee and rolls. As they huddled around the small kitchen table, Evie posed her question to Mrs. Olson about the comings and goings next door.

"It was just Allen and Crystal, at first," Mrs. Olson said. "The other girls moved in this past fall." A look of realization came over her face. "I suppose that was what Crystal meant when she said something about how it just wasn't right when there was more than the two of them."

Mrs. Olson glanced nervously at Mr. Olson who was scowling and briskly stirring his coffee.

"I should have run him off when I first saw him. No good! I could see it the minute I laid eyes on him," he said.

"No need to get excited, dear," Mrs. Olson said. "He's gone, now."

"What's all this about?" Gary asked.

Beth and Evie gave him a short recap.

Evie finished up, "So, we wondered if the fight between Al and Crystal happened because the two other girls moved in. And, it sounds like that fits."

"I see. So, she tried to run off before. Maybe, this time she made it. Anyway, they're all gone, now that their house burned down. Case closed," Gary said. He pushed back his chair. "Let's get going. People are waiting for a tow. Are you girls ready?"

Everyone bustled around. The girls effusively thanked their hosts while wrapping up to face the cold. Mrs. Olson pressed a bag of sweet rolls into Beth's hands.

Soon, Gary, Beth, and Evie were in the cab of Gary's tow truck, with Beth in the middle. Her car trailed behind. The truck ground, slowly, through the thick snow. Here and there, snow was drifted into mounds, across the road. Then, Gary drove on the other side of the road, following the tracks he'd made when coming to the Olson's house.

Beth said to Gary, "I think Sam knows something about Crystal's disappearance and the fire."

"Why do you say that?" he asked.

"We saw him driving toward Davison City yesterday, on our way out here," Beth said.

"What of it? He could have been coming from Grand Bend."

"He could have, but one of Al's girls heard an argument between Al and another man, just before the fire started. She knows Sam and she recognized his voice," Beth said.

Gary whistled in amazement. "He did seem kind of wound up when he came to work yesterday. But, I didn't talk to him. I was pretty ticked off at him for missing work without calling in." He slowed down to turn onto the highway. The highway had been plowed and, once on it, Gary sped up. "We should be back to town in fifteen to twenty minutes. I'll drop you off first, Evie, and then you Beth. Okay?"

They agreed.

"So, Sam was out there, and he got into a fight with Al. I wonder why," Gary said.

"Because of Crystal," Evie said. "Sarah and Dawn only heard part of the fight, when it got loud. But it sounds like Sam wanted to know where she was. He seemed to think that Al knew, and he was trying to force him to tell."

"But you know she's dead. You still believe that. Right, Beth?" Gary asked.

"Right," Beth said, slowly.

"According to Sarah, Al screamed something about throwing Crystal out," Evie said.

"Which is kind of odd. Did he mean he threw her out, so she went to the train station to leave town, or what?" Beth said. "I bet Sarah and Dawn know more than they're saying. I wish we had another chance to ask them questions. I wonder where they are now."

As they approached where the highway turned south and went into Davison City, they saw tire tracks leading to a steep drop-off to the river. A car perched near the edge of the hill, its tail end pointing toward them. It looked like the driver had been going too fast to make the turn. Luckily, the deep snow had slowed him enough to prevent him from driving over the edge. A man got out of the car and waved his arms to get their attention.

"Looks like he needs a tow. As you can see, I've got my work cut out for me." Gary pulled over and parked. "I'll just talk to him for a minute, and tell him how soon I can be back."

That task accomplished, Gary drove into town and dropped Evie off.

"Come over later for rolls and tea," Beth said to her. Raising the bag Mrs. Olson had given her."

"Sure, if I can. I'll give you a call and let you know," Evie said.

Gary took Beth home, maneuvered her car into its parking spot, and plugged it in.

"Thanks a ton, Gary. It's great having a superhero for a brother. Want to come in for a few minutes?"

"No thanks. Got to get back to work. Just try to stay out of trouble for a day or two, okay? I need to get some sleep," he said. He climbed back into his tow truck and roared off to rescue other stranded motorists.

Beth let herself in through the back door into the kitchen. Chestnut was nowhere in sight. She took off her wraps, dumped them into a heap, and got the box of kitty food out of the cupboard. "Here, kitty, kitty," she called as she poured some into his bowl.

Chestnut stalked into the kitchen, back arched and tail erect, clearly annoyed by the lateness of his meal, but unable to resist the invitation. He ignored her and went straight to his food dish.

Chapter 24

To get rid of the lingering scent of smoke from yesterday's house fire, Beth took a long soak in the tub and washed her hair.

"I'll have to write an apology letter to Mrs. Olson," she told Chestnut, who sat on the bath mat keeping an eye on her. "She probably had to wash all the bedding, and air out the bedroom, to get rid of the smoky odor."

He looked at her with interest, as though considering her comment.

Wrapped up in a robe and slippers, with a towel around her head, Beth returned to the kitchen just as her phone began to ring. *It must be Evie*, she thought. She grabbed up the receiver.

"Are you coming over?" she asked.

"What? Hello? Is this Beth Williams?" An unknown woman's voice asked.

"Oh, I'm sorry. Yes, this is Beth. I was expecting someone else. Who's calling?"

"This is Donna. I was given your number by Marsha Johnson. She said you called her about Crystal."

"Oh, yes, I've been trying to get in touch with you."

"Sorry about that. We've been out of town for a few days. Marsha said you're a friend of Crystal's and you're looking for her. Is that right?"

Beth hesitated, then said, "Yes, I'm looking for her," she said. "Has she contacted you, lately?"

"No, not lately. We were in touch before Christmas. She was planning to come to the cities and I was supposed to pick her up at the train station, but her plans must have changed. She didn't show up. Have you seen her since?"

"No, I last saw her on the evening of December 21st."

"Really? That's when she was supposed to take the train. Where did you see her?"

"Near the train station," Beth said.

"Near it? This is all very odd. She must have changed her mind. But, why? Did you talk to her?"

"Well...Perhaps I should tell you a bit more. But first, let me ask you, were you very close to Crystal?"

"Close? Not really. You see, we have the same dad but different mothers. My dad only told me about Crystal a couple of years ago. He wanted to get in touch with her—to make amends—after Crystal's mom passed away. He had a fling with her mom, and then Crystal was born. When he found out about the pregnancy, he was already engaged to my mom, so he didn't acknowledge her. It sounds awful, I know, but that's what happened."

"I see. So, after he told you about Crystal, you two met?"

"Just a few times. Crystal was living in foster care and had a boyfriend who took up a lot of her time. Allen somebody. I think she ran away with him, in the end."

"Allen Peterson?" Beth asked.

"Yes, that's right. I only met him once, and didn't much like him. Anyway, even though Crystal and I didn't have a lot in common, I liked her and I felt sorry for her. So, I was happy when she got in touch and said she was coming to the cities. I got the impression that she was thinking of moving here, permanently. Maybe she got tired of Allen. Do you suppose he stopped her?"

"I think that's quite possible," Beth said.

They talked a while longer. Beth promised to let her know if she found Crystal, and hung up. Within moments of hanging up, the phone rang again.

"I've been trying to get hold of you," Evie said. She sounded out of breath.

"I was on the phone with Donna, Crystal's half-sister. She said—"

"Never mind that, now. They've found the body," Evie said.

"What?"

"They found Crystal's body. I'm coming over. I'll be right there," Evie said, and rang off.

Beth jumped into a pair of jeans, a sweatshirt, and wooly socks. She was in her bedroom, blow-drying her hair when she was interrupted by a loud knock. Beth rushed to the door and let Evie in. Her cheeks were bright red from the cold and her blue eyes sparkled with excitement.

"You said they found the body. Who found it? Where?" Beth asked.

"In the culvert, just outside of town. You know, where the highway turns west toward Grand Bend. Your brother nearly stepped on her while he was hooking up a car that had gone off the road—the one he stopped at this morning. Just think, she was there this whole time. We must have driven past her a dozen times."

"Oh, my God! You're right," Beth said. "Are the police there now?"

"Yeah, Gary called them and met them there. Then he tried to call you. When he couldn't get through, he called me. Do you want to go?"

Beth hesitated. She felt a little squeamish as she pictured Crystal. "Do you think we should? The cops must have that area cordoned off. Where would we park? Can we even get close?"

"Good point, but we could just go and see. Maybe we can park on the shoulder."

"Okay, but I have to dry my hair. It'll just take a few minutes. Come and talk to me while I finish."

Evie followed Beth into the bedroom and perched on the edge of the bed. She had on her puffy jacket, and Chestnut saw it as a comfy place for a nap. He jumped up beside her and started kneading a spot on her lap. Beth and Evie raised their voices to be heard over the roar of the hairdryer.

"So Gary found Crystal. That's wild," Beth said. "If he hadn't towed that car, she might have lain there covered by snow until spring. What did he say about it?"

"He was pretty freaked out. Naturally. He kept saying, 'She's dead. She's really dead.' Like he finally believed it. Until now, I don't think he was sure," Evie said.

"I don't blame him. I was starting to doubt it, myself. After telling so many people Crystal was just stunned and then wandered off, I sort of half-believed it. How about you? Did you believe she was dead?"

"I did and I didn't. It's so surreal. You know? I mean, people don't just go around killing other people, at least not in Davison City. It's not like we're living in Chicago or New York."

Chestnut jumped off Evie's lap and hid under the bed.

"What was that all about?" Evie said.

Beth turned off the hairdryer and then heard a loud knock on the door. That must have been what frightened Chestnut.

"I'll see who it is," Evie said as she headed to the door.

Beth heard Evie say, "Oh, it's you." A low, male voice answered. She stuck her head out of the bedroom, hairbrush in one hand, and saw Bill Crample—large and out of place—standing on her doormat.

He nodded in her direction. "Miss Williams," he said.

So formal—this must be an official call, Beth thought.

"Hi Officer Crample," she said.

She ducked back into the bedroom and dropped the brush next to the hairdryer on her dresser, then joined Evie and Bill Crample in the living room.

"What brings you here?" she asked him.

He gave her a skeptical look.

"I imagine you already know. This morning your brother found the body of a young woman who meets the description of a person you reported dead a couple of weeks ago. But, in a location different from the one you indicated at that time."

"I see. So, Crystal is dead, as I originally reported. Not missing, as you supposed."

His ears, already red from the cold, darkened a shade, but his expression remained impassive and his voice was unchanged.

"I'd like you to come with me, and see if she is the woman you reported," he said.

"Well, I certainly hope she is. It's unlikely that two women would have been killed within the past few weeks."

Bill Crample gave her a forced smile. "So, if you are ready."

"Right now?"

"Yes, right now. That is…your help would be appreciated."

Beth tried to read his expression, but he was all business.

"If Evie can come along." She turned to Evie. "Do you want to come with us?"

"Sure," Evie said.

"Fine. I'll be out in my squad car. Come on out when you're ready." He glanced at her hair.

Beth reached up and touched her hair, and realized that static electricity must be making it stick up at odd angles. Now, she was embarrassed. She felt her cheeks grow hot.

"What a jerk," she said after he'd closed the door behind him.

Evie chuckled. "Don't worry about it. Anyway, he's the one who burst in on us."

Beth dashed back into the bedroom, sprayed a cloud of hairspray around to tone down the frizz, and then slipped on a wide hairband. *My hair will be a mess after I take off my winter hat, anyway,* she thought as she cast one last, despairing glance at her image in the mirror. Then she bundled up and followed Evie out to the squad car. Bill let them into the back seat and started the drive out to the edge of town.

"Are you the investigator?" Beth asked him once they were underway.

"Me? No way. I'm just a patrol cop. Our investigator, Captain Swensen, is in charge. I'm just here because I filled out the initial report. I told him what little I know. He sent me to pick you up."

A few minutes later, they arrived. The westbound lane of the highway was blocked by traffic cones and squad cars with their lights blinking. Those, and other official vehicles, were parked on the road. Fortunately, since it was a Sunday, there wasn't much traffic. Most people were in church or still digging out from last night's snowstorm. Bill Crample's squad car was waved through by one of the policemen, who were directing traffic, and then he parked.

Beth said to Evie, "I guess we'll have to miss church today. Hopefully, Father McClure won't notice."

"I think we have a good excuse," Evie said. "I hope he asks. That would be a chance to talk to him again." Evie gave Beth a significant look.

Beth looked up and saw Bill watching them in the rearview mirror. *He certainly doesn't miss much*, she thought, annoyed by his eavesdropping.

He got out of the car and opened the back door on the driver's side, and Evie and Beth got out, too.

"This way," he said. He led them to a man in civilian clothes, who was talking to a uniformed officer and introduced them to the middle-aged, balding man with earmuffs covering his ears. "Captain, these are the girls I told you about. This is Beth Williams, and her friend, Evie Hanson."

"How do you do?" he nodded toward them. "I understand one of you reported seeing the girl when she was killed. Which one of you was that?"

"That was me. I'm Beth Williams."

"Okay. Can you take a look for me and see if you recognize this girl?"

Beth nodded.

"I'll wait up here," Evie said.

The captain led the way down the bank of the ravine, slipping on the trampled snow in his rubber overshoes. They stopped in front of a pile of debris—the worn arm of an orange sofa stuck out of it—partially cleared of snow. In front of the pile lay a black tarp. The captain nodded to an officer, who pulled back the tarp, revealing the victim.

Beth stared at Crystal, the girl she'd been searching for and thinking about for the past two weeks. Her hair was full of snow. Her eyes, still open, had clouded over so now, they were almost as pale as the surrounding snow. Her skin had turned a blue-gray shade. She looked different, but it was definitely her. A chain with a medal on it dangled from around her neck. Beth bent over to get a better look. It was a St. Michael the Archangel medal.

"Don't touch her," the captain barked.

Beth drew back her hand. "I won't," she said, straightening up.

"It's just that we might find fibers or other evidence on the body. So we don't want it disturbed. Is that the girl you saw?" Captain Swensen said.

Beth nodded mutely. She felt that if she spoke, her voice might break and she would begin to cry. Bill Crample reached out, took her arm, and helped her back up the hill. The captain followed them.

"Are you okay," Bill asked.

"Yes, I'm fine." Beth pulled her arm away and shook her head to dislodge the image of Crystal's face. "It was just... I don't know. She looked so dead."

"Not very nice, is it?" the captain said. He turned to Officer Crample. "Take the girls back to the station, give them something hot to drink, and get a statement. I'll be back after I'm done here." He turned and walked away.

Chapter 25

"Tomorrow we go back to school," Evie said. They were in Beth's kitchen, having a late lunch of peanut butter and jelly sandwiches and sweet rolls. She took a big bite out of one of Mrs. Olson's rolls. "Umm, these are delicious."

"I know," Beth said and licked frosting from her fingers. "It will seem pretty anticlimactic to sit in a classroom and listen to a professor drone on, after what we've been through these past two weeks," Beth said.

"At least we have some closure, after finding her body," Evie said.

"True. But, I dread making those phone calls," Beth said.

"You mean to Crystal's family," Evie said.

"Yeah. I wish I had better news. I also wish I could tell them we know who did it," Beth said.

"Seems like it was Allen, don't you think?" Evie said. "After all, he was furious at her for running out on him and he'd gotten violent with her in the past."

"True. But, I'm not so sure," Beth said.

"Why's that?" Evie asked.

"Al dropped Crystal off at the Big Boy. Right? Then someone else picked her up. So, whoever that was, he was the last person to see her alive."

"Or, maybe nobody picked her up," Evie said. "Maybe Allen killed her because she was running away and he never did drop her off at the Big Boy."

"How would that work?" Beth asked. "How would she get to the railroad station? She couldn't call a cab from home with Allen, Sarah, and Dawn around. But, I suppose if Allen did drop her off at the restaurant, she could have taken a cab from there to the railroad station after he left."

"Or, someone could have given her a ride," Evie said.

"You're right," Beth said. "But who was it? It could have been Sam, he had a thing for her. Or, maybe it was Father McClure. He was late for mass that Saturday night. Remember? Come on, let's finish up here, and head out. We have time to ask a few more questions this afternoon."

"Hang on. Before we dash off, let's stop and think. Who else should we question besides Sam and Father McClure? Maybe we should go back to the Big Boy and ask around. Someone may have noticed Crystal there that night," Evie said.

"True. And, we need to talk to the men who we know had picked up Crystal from the Big Boy. Besides Sam, that was the banker, Mr. Brown, and the lawyer, Mr. Nobis."

"That's turning into a long list of suspects," Evie said. "We don't have time to question them all today. I need to be home for supper. Jim might call tonight and I don't want to miss him. In murder mysteries, the detective usually gets everyone together to question them. I suppose it doesn't work that way in real life."

"Not for us. Unless…" Beth trailed off.

"Unless, what? Are your little gray cells firing up?" Evie said.

Beth laughed. "No, I wish I was as clever as Poirot. My gray cells are as dormant as ever. I was just thinking, maybe I could ask Miss Tanner to throw another get-together for the library supporters. That would get some of the suspects together, including the banker, the lawyer, and the priest. Meanwhile, let's talk to Sam and the staff at the Big Boy. Before we do, let's write everything down, in the order it happened." Beth went to get a pencil and a notebook. Settled back at the kitchen table, pencil poised, she said, "What happened first?"

"Well, you found the body on the way to work. Right?"

Beth wrote down, 4:00 p.m., December 21, 1968. Next to it, she wrote, "Discovered Crystal's body. Talked to the police."

Beth sat back and stared at the page for a moment. "Oh, my God! I'm so stupid."

"What?" Evie asked.

"The time. Look at the time. Four o'clock."

"Yeah, so?"

"So, we've been thinking it was in the evening. But it wasn't evening. It was in the afternoon. Every other time that we know of, when someone picked up Crystal or another one of Al's girls from the Big Boy, it was always in the evening. When we did our stakeout and saw Al drop Dawn off and Sam pick her up, we were there at supper time. So this was different. We've been asking the wrong people. We need to ask the afternoon staff if they saw Crystal there that day."

"You're right. Let's go to the Big Boy and talk to the afternoon staff," Evie said.

They got there around 2:00 p.m. A snowplow was still clearing the parking lot, which was mostly empty. If there had been a lunch rush, it was over.

They asked for the manager, and a burly man, his shirt straining against a large belly, came out from the back.

"Can I help you, girls?" he said with a forced smile.

"We have some questions. Do you have time to talk?" Beth said.

"Is there a problem? he asked."

"No, no problem," Beth said. "Not yet, anyway."

His smile faded as he scrutinized them, then he gestured for them to follow him. "Come on back."

He led them to a stained door, warped at the bottom, opened it, and led them into what appeared to be a combination storage room and office. He walked behind the desk and sat down, heavily, in a swivel chair.

"Okay. State your business. I'm busy," he said, not bothering to offer them a seat.

His manner annoyed Beth.

"We want to talk to your afternoon staff and ask them some questions. Do we have your permission?" Evie asked.

"No, you don't have my permission," he said, with emphasis on "permission." "They have work to do. Why do you want to?"

"A girl died. Maybe you heard about it," Beth said. "Her name was Crystal Jones. She was last seen here. We think some of your staff might know something about it. Maybe you know something about it yourself."

He glared at Beth. "I don't know anything about it, and I don't appreciate your insinuations. So, beat it, before I call the cops." He reached for the phone.

She decided to call his bluff. "Go ahead, call them. Ask for Bill Crample. I think he'd be very interested in your little arrangement."

"What arrangement?" he asked, but he pulled his hand back from the phone.

"The one you have with Al Peterson—where you look the other way as he uses this restaurant as a drop-off and pickup point for his, shall we say, trade?"

Beads of sweat collected on the fat man's forehead. He pulled a graying, rumpled handkerchief out of his pants pocket and mopped his brow.

"By the way, your arrangement with Al might be a thing of the past since his place just burned down. Did you know that? So, you might want to hang onto your job. I think the Big Boy management might be very interested in what's been going on here."

"I don't mean to be uncooperative. I just wondered why you're asking, that's all," he said.

"We're her friends," Evie said.

"Oh, I see. In that case," he harrumphed. "I suppose there's no harm in asking a few questions. Just be discrete. Don't talk to the girls while they're in the dining room."

"Thanks, we appreciate it," Beth said. "If you want to ask the staff to come on back here, we can get this over with quickly."

He scurried off to do as she asked.

"Wow, I'm impressed," Evie said. "When did you get so tough?"

Beth laughed. "I'm just glad he bought it. I wasn't sure if there was an arrangement, or not, until I saw his reaction. I was doing an impression of a tough cop, as seen on TV, crossed with my best mean librarian persona that I use when dealing with angry patrons who don't want to pay for books they've lost."

The staff wandered in, and Beth passed around a picture, gave a description of what she was wearing, and asked if anyone remembered seeing her on the afternoon of December 21st. Most of them said no, shrugged, or shook their heads.

The fry cook looked thoughtful and said, "I might have seen her using the payphone around 3:00 that day. The phone is right across from the kitchen. I noticed her as I put an order up under the lights. She caught my eye because of her long dress, which was out of the ordinary. I thought that maybe she was going to a Christmas party or something. I didn't see who dropped her off or picked her up, though."

Beth and Evie thanked the staff and left without speaking to the manager.

"It sounds like she was here that afternoon," Beth said. "Not that that helps much. We have a time, but we still don't know who dropped her off, or who picked her up."

"There's one thing we do know," Evie said.

"What's that?" Beth asked.

"We're going to have to find a new place to eat. I'm not sure we'll be welcome here after today," Evie said.

They laughed their way back to the car.

"Now, let's go find out what Sam has to say," Beth said.

Chapter 26

"Let me see if I've got it straight," Evie said as Beth drove from the Big Boy to Gary's auto repair shop. "Crystal called someone from the Big Boy pay phone on the afternoon of December 21st. And, that person gave her a ride to the train station."

"Seems like it," Beth said.

"Maybe she took a cab," Evie said.

"That's easy to check. Shall we stop by and ask?" Beth asked.

"Yeah, let's do that. It's not far out of our way," Evie said.

There wasn't much call for cabs in Davison City. The only cab in town was a mom-and-pop operation. One antiquated cab was parked in front of the tiny office, on Second Street. Beth stayed in the car while Evie popped in and asked if there had been any fares from the Big Boy restaurant, on the afternoon of December 21st. There hadn't been. So, that meant Crystal had called someone to get a ride to the train station.

Back in the car, Evie said, "One thing puzzles me."

"What's that?" Beth asked.

"Suppose she was dropped off by Al, as usual. But, instead of waiting for her customer to pick her up, she makes a phone call and splits," Evie said.

"Right, so far. Outside of the unusual time of day, there's nothing strange about that," Beth said.

"I don't know. The timing doesn't fit. Wouldn't the customer arrive pretty soon after Al dropped her off? If he did, she'd still be there, waiting for her ride, and he'd see her leave with someone else."

"You're right," Beth exclaimed.

"Hey, watch it!" Evie said. "You just ran through that red light."

"Oh, sorry," Beth said. "You're blowing my mind. Don't come up with any other great insights while I drive, okay."

"I'll try not to," Evie said. "And, these customers pay up front, right? So, if they arrive and their 'date' isn't waiting, wouldn't they call Al and ask for their money back or another girl?"

"Yeah, that's another good point," Beth said.

"Well, we're here. Let's see what Sam has to say," Beth said as they pulled into the parking lot of the auto repair shop and stopped.

Inside, Sam looked haggard. He sat at the desk, his head propped up on his hands. He was unshaven and there were dark rings under his eyes.

"Oh, hi," he said. He sounded tired. "Gary's not here. He's still out towing and starting cars."

"That's okay. We wanted to talk to you. Got a minute?" Beth said.

"Sure." He shrugged. "The phone has stopped ringing non-stop. What's up?"

Beth looked around and realized that the only chairs, besides the one Sam occupied, were the ones up against the window in the waiting area. "Why don't you roll your chair over here, so we can have a chat," she said.

He looked a little leery and looked at Evie, who smiled in encouragement.

"What's this all about?" he said as he wheeled his chair around the desk and over to them."

They all sat down.

"We saw you yesterday, out on the highway. You were heading toward town when we were heading out," Evie said.

"Yeah, so?" he said.

"Did you see us?" she asked.

"Nope. I must have been watching the road," he said.

"We were wondering," Evie said. "Where were you coming from?"

"Grand Bend, I guess. What do you care? Since when are you keeping track of me?"

"It's just that you'd been missing for a couple of days," Beth said. "According to Gary, you were supposed to be at work, but you weren't. We all wondered what had happened to you, and then, there you were."

"Yeah, I guess I lost track of time. You know how it goes." He threw a sidelong glance at Evie. "Anyway, I already told Gary I was sorry about missing work. He's okay with it."

"Well, that's great," Beth said. "But we happen to know you didn't spend all your time in Grand Bend."

Sam stiffened. "What do you mean?"

"I mean, we talked to Sarah and Dawn, and we know you fought with Al," Beth said. "So, we'd like you to tell us about that. Did you know their house burned down after you left? Did you start the fire?"

He stared at her, mouth open, for a moment. "No, I didn't start the fire. I didn't even know there was a fire. Was anyone hurt?"

"Nope. Well, Al got a little singed, but he walked away from it okay. Dawn and Sarah got out before he did, but all their stuff got burned up," Beth said.

"Wow! That's too bad," he said. "But, I had nothing to do with it. You gotta believe me."

"Why were you out there, Sam?" Evie asked softly.

Sam rubbed his face, and then dropped his hands, limply, into his lap. "It was stupid. I shouldn't have gone out there."

"We all do things we shouldn't do. Go ahead. Tell us what happened," Evie said.

"Okay. So, when my little brother came home a couple of weeks ago and said the lady at the library had seen a dead girl, I didn't pay much attention. He's always coming up with crazy stuff. You know how kids are."

"That's true," Evie said.

"But then, the next weekend I met up with Dawn—you know—and she said something about Crystal being missing."

"Was that the night we saw you driving the Pontiac?" Beth asked.

"Yeah, it was. I know I shouldn't have taken that car. But, I didn't see any harm in it. It was just sitting here. When I saw Evie's car following me, I panicked. I didn't want Gary to find out."

"That's okay," Evie said. "Gary knows now and I'm sure he'll get over it. Just don't do it again. So, then what happened?"

"A few more days went by and Gary asked me about the car and said you and Beth are looking into Crystal's disappearance. Then, I remembered that Bobby said you found a dead girl, not that some girl was missing." Sam hesitated.

"And then what?" Evie prompted.

"I wasn't sure what to do next. I liked Crystal. You know? I mean, she was just a, a—"

"A call girl," Beth said.

"Yeah, that, but she was nice. We'd talk some, after—you know—and I kind of liked her. I didn't like to think of her just lying out in the snow, somewhere, dead. So I wanted to talk to Allen about it."

"So, what day was that?" Beth asked.

"I meant to drive out there on Thursday," Sam said. "I know, I was supposed to go to work. But, I decided that this was more important."

"That was Thursday. But, it was actually Saturday when you went out there, wasn't it?" Beth said.

"Yeah. I meant to go straight out there. But, first, I went to the Pig and Whistle, to get a drink. To steady my nerves, you know."

"Sure, that makes sense," Evie said. "Then what happened?"

"After a couple of drinks, I was going to leave, but my truck wouldn't start. Then, I went back into the bar and hung around with some friends, you know. After closing time, it turned into a big house party, and I sort of lost track of time. Eventually, I got my truck going and then I drove out to Al's place."

"That was on Saturday. Right?" Beth asked. "When we saw you driving back home."

"Yeah, that was Saturday. And, I fought with Al, but it didn't start the fire. And, I sure didn't kill Crystal."

"Tell us what happened," Evie said.

"Okay. Al was alone when I got there, at least I didn't see anyone else around. He opened the door and tried to be all pally-wally, offered me a beer and stuff," Sam said.

"Did you have one?" Evie asked.

"No way. I said I wasn't there for a beer, and he'd better tell me what happened to Crystal. Right away, he got belligerent and started shouting he didn't know and didn't care, and stuff like that. He tried to throw me out. I punched him once, and he went down like a sack of potatoes. There was a clang. I guess he hit his head on something. I didn't stick around to find out. I took off. I have no idea what happened next."

"One thing puzzles me," Beth said. "How did you know where Al lived? I mean, didn't he always drop off his girls at the Big Boy."

"Naw. I always knew where he lived. This whole drop-off business only started recently. I guess he wanted to keep things cool with his neighbors, or something."

The phone rang and Sam went to answer it and wrote something down.

"Did you hear that?" Beth said quietly to Evie. "He was at the Pig and Whistle on Thursday."

"Yeah, so?" Evie said.

"So that's over by the railroad station, isn't it?" Beth said.

"You're right. Are you going to ask him about it, or should I?" Evie said.

"You should. He seems to open up to you," Beth said.

Sam came back and sat down. "Another car that won't start. But, they're going to have to wait. We have a whole long list of people ahead of them."

Evie said, "You were at the Pig and Whistle. That's such a fun place. Remember when Jim and I ran into you there, and you two played darts. You won, as I recall."

Sam smiled at the recollection. "Yeah, I play a lot of darts there, but I don't usually win. I guess I got lucky that night."

"That's right across from the train station, isn't it?" Evie asked.

"Yes, it is," he said.

"Did you happen to notice anything out of the ordinary?" Evie said.

He stopped to think. "Now that you mention it, I did. Yeah. One Saturday, a couple weeks ago, I was parking my truck and I saw Father McClure's car. I wondered what he was doing there."

"Are you sure it was his car?" Beth asked.

"Yeah, I have a pretty good memory when it comes to cars, and it had his rosary hanging from the rearview mirror," he said.

"What time was that?" Beth asked.

"It was close to 4:00. I remember because I looked at my watch and thought, "Wow, he's cutting it close. He's going to be late for mass.""

Chapter 27

After their conversation with Sam, Beth dropped Evie off at home and made a beeline to Our Lady of Sorrows church. She had some questions for Father McClure. She parked in the church parking lot—her car was the only one there—and followed the sidewalk to the side door of the church. It was locked. She went around to the front and up the stairs. After trying a couple of doors, she found an open one and entered into the hushed quiet of the empty church.

It took a moment for her eyes to adjust to the semi-darkness of the vestibule. She pushed her way through the swinging doors and entered the main body of the church. The late evening light slanted through the stained glass windows, throwing patterns of colored light across the pews. She dipped the fingers of her right hand into the holy water font, and crossed herself, as she mentally nodded hello to the brightly colored statues standing on either side of the altar.

She had hoped that she would find Father McClure here, after Sunday vespers, so she wouldn't have to go to the rectory and face his formidable housekeeper, Mrs. Karpova. But, he wasn't there.

A basket of religious items for sale, which sat on a table at the back of the church among piles of publications, bulletins, and holy cards, caught her eye. A small sign next to the basket read $1 each. A wooden box with a slot in the top, marked "donations," sat on the other side of the sign. She picked up one of the little, plastic boxes out of the basket. It contained a holy medal of St. Patrick on a chain. Other boxes contained medals of other saints or rosaries.

At that moment, an image sprang to mind of Crystal passing her in the church vestibule. She was looking down, not making eye contact with her, as she left the church one afternoon. In her mind's eye, she watched Crystal open the door and go out. The trees on the boulevard were yellow. It was fall.

So that was why Crystal had seemed familiar when she saw her lying at the bottom of the hill in Central Park, Beth thought.

"Those are nice, aren't they,"

Father McClure's voice, behind her, made her jump.

"Oh, I'm sorry, Beth. I didn't mean to startle you. If you're here for vespers, I'm afraid you're too late." Father McClure smiled at her.

"No, I'm not," she said. Beth's heart thumped against her breastbone. "I was...I was just looking for you. And then I noticed these. Have these always been here?"

"Well, I don't know about always. Always is a long time. But for a while, yes. Is there something in particular that you'd like? We seem to have quite a selection. The basket must have been recently restocked." He rooted through it as he talked. "A rosary, or a medal of your patron saint, perhaps. I'm sorry, I don't remember your birthdate. I should remember. But, there are so many more of you than there are of me." He chuckled.

"No, I…How about a St. Michael the Archangel medal? That would be nice. If there is one."

Beth pawed through her purse for change and put it into the offerings box.

"Perhaps. Let's see." Father McClure continued his search. "They are quite popular, you know. But, we might get lucky. Oh yes, here's one."

He held up his find and then handed it to her. Beth exchanged it for the one in her hand, which she returned to the basket.

"You were looking for me, you said. Was there something in particular you wanted to talk to me about?" he said.

"I just wanted to explain why I missed mass this morning," Beth said.

"That's quite understandable. Many of the parishioners didn't make it today. I'm sure you would have if you could. You have always been very faithful."

"Thank you, Father. I just wanted to explain. You see, Evie and I were out of town yesterday, and we got caught in the storm. We didn't make it back until this morning."

"Evie Hanson? Such a nice girl. Well, as I said, it is perfectly understandable under the circumstances."

"Yes, well, as I was saying," Beth pressed on, feeling a bit frustrated that he was keeping her from getting to the rest of her explanation. "You see, I was picked up by the police once I got home."

"Picked up by the police? But, why?"

"Do you remember when Evie and I came to the rectory?"

"I do, and I want to apologize for any misunderstanding. I hope it didn't cause any ill will."

It took Beth a moment to figure out what he was talking about, and then remembered the "friend" she invented, who supposedly wanted to convert, and the aftermath.

"No, no, that's quite all right. I meant the girl we asked you about—Crystal Jones. We showed you a sketch. Do you recall?"

"Oh yes," his smile fell. "I heard from some parishioners that she was found this afternoon. Very sad. Yes, very sad, indeed. The things people do to each other. It's shocking. Quite shocking—"

He seemed poised to go on in this vein for some time.

Beth interrupted, "Did you know her?"

"No, I wouldn't say that I knew her," he said.

"I remember, that's what you said when we first asked. Only, you must have known her fairly well, because you drove twenty miles out to the Olson's house to pick her up."

His smile faded. "How do you know that?"

"Mrs. Olson told me. Evie and I stopped there yesterday during the storm. They invited us to stay overnight until it cleared up, and we got to talking. She told me how Crystal had walked to their house last fall after a fight with her boyfriend, and then called you."

He sighed heavily and sat down in the last pew. He motioned her over. "Won't you join me?"

Beth sat down next to him.

"Yes, it's true. I did know her. I was attempting to be discrete—not one of my strong suits, as you know. She came to the church one day last fall and introduced herself. She told me a bit about her and her, um, her living arrangements. She said her mother had been Catholic, so she had been baptized, but that was about the extent of her religious background. I was attempting to help her find a better way of life. I'm sorry that it was cut short." He sighed again. "But, what is your interest in her?"

"I was the one who found her after she'd been killed," Beth said.

"You? But I thought it was your brother who called the police," he said.

"Not today. I saw her, dead, in Central Park, the Saturday before Christmas." Beth told him what had happened. "But, her body disappeared before the police got there, and it was finally found today."

"I see. Yes. I hadn't put it all together. As I recall, you said you were looking for her, and that she was missing. But, she was dead all along," he said.

"Yes, I did say that. When the police didn't find her body, they concluded that she wasn't dead, just missing, and I went along with their version. I was halfway convinced of it myself, until today."

"Yes, yes, that must have been very shocking for you," he said. "To find a body, like that. Naturally, it was quite unexpected." He sat silently and absorbed the information. "So, now you are looking for who killed her. Is that right?"

Beth's heart began to beat faster as she realized that she was sitting, alone, with the man who might have killed Crystal. But, she had known Father McClure her whole life. Surely, he wasn't a killer. She had to ask.

"You were late to mass that Saturday night and your car was seen outside of the train station, close to 4:00 that evening. What were you doing there?" she said.

He turned and stared at her for a moment. "You are asking me if I killed her?"

"No…no…I didn't think that…"

"No, but you're wondering. It's quite natural. I knew the girl. I hid my relationship with her. I was seen at the time and place she was last known to be alive. But, no, I did not kill her," he said bitterly. "I gave her a ride to the train station, that's all."

"I'm sorry, Father. I shouldn't have even…"

He waved aside her apology and continued his story. "Crystal had finally decided that she was leaving her life here behind. I believe she'd reconnected with some family members and arranged to make her escape. I don't know the details. I just got a phone call from her, picked her up from the Big Boy, and dropped her at the station."

"So, you didn't see her off," she said.

"No. I wish to God I had. I could have prevented this tragedy. But, I was late for mass as it was. I just walked her to the door of the station, and said goodbye," he said.

"So, that's how the cuffs of your pants got wet," Beth mused.

"What?"

"Just a detail that was mentioned. Someone told me that you were late to mass and that the cuffs of your pants, seen below your cassock, were wet.

"Oh, yes," he said. "Your source, whoever that is, is certainly observant. Yes, I had to step into the snow getting in and out of my car at the railroad station, and I hadn't taken the time to put on boots. They should do a better job shoveling."

Chapter 28

It was Tuesday, the second day of winter quarter. Beth and Evie sat in the Student Union cafeteria and compared notes over lunch.

"How do you like your new classes," Evie asked, poking at her salad. She pointed at Beth's tray. "What's that?"

"Tacos. They're good. But they're tricky to eat. No matter how I do it, it's messy," Beth said. She demonstrated, holding a taco, sideways, and tilting her head as she took a bite. Part of the taco broke off and fell back onto her plate. She grabbed a couple of paper napkins and wiped taco sauce off of her fingers.

"My classes are okay, so far. You know how it goes—they pass out the syllabuses and talk about them. Same old stuff—grad school or undergrad. How about you, how do you like your classes?"

"Good, it's mostly art. I got stuck with a late afternoon class, thanks to my last-minute schedule change. Other than that, I can't complain," Evie said.

"Too bad we have such different schedules this quarter. It was nice when we could take turns driving."

"True. By the way, how did the phone calls go?" Evie asked.

"You mean to Crystal's family?" Beth said. "They were kind of rough. The one to her half-sister wasn't too bad. She wasn't that close to Crystal. I think she half-expected something like that might have happened when Crystal didn't show up or call. The one to her foster mom was worse. She kept crying."

"That sounds brutal. What about the foster sister, did you talk to her?"

"Yeah, I stopped by yesterday and talked to her in person, since I was passing by and she seemed to have been very fond of Crystal." Beth grimaced. "She took it kind of hard."

"I'm sorry you had to go through that," Evie said.

"That's okay. My choice. I could have let the cops handle it, I suppose. But, who knows when they might have gotten around to it. I didn't want to leave them hanging."

"Did you tell them who did it?" Evie asked.

"No, because I'm not sure. Of course, they suspect Allen. Everyone does," Beth said. "And, maybe he did it. Did you hear? He split from the hospital before he was discharged before they could arrest him."

"No way. When did this happen?"

"I don't know when he left the hospital, but Crample called and told me about it this morning," Beth said. "He wanted to alert me. In case I see him lurking around town."

"I told you Bill likes you," Evie said.

Beth said, "Yeah? Well, I don't like him. Can you imagine having a big, dumb lug like him for a boyfriend?"

"I suppose he could come in handy from time to time." Evie wiggled her eyebrows suggestively.

This sent them both into a fit of giggles.

"Oh, before I forget," Beth said, after she regained her composure. "Miss Tanner agreed to have a special Library Supporters get-together at her house, on the 19th. Can you come?"

"Absolutely, I wouldn't miss it. That's a Sunday. Right?" Evie said as she dug her calendar out of her backpack.

"Right. And, it's Edgar Allen Poe's birthday, which appealed to Miss Tanner's quirky sense of humor. When I asked her if she would set up a Library Supporters meeting so I could get some of our suspects together, she picked the day and is sending out the invitations. We'll see who shows up."

"This sounds exciting. What time is it going to be?" Evie said.

"Three o'clock," Beth said.

Evie jotted it down on her calendar.

On Thursday, Beth stopped by the college library to pick up a stack of books for Mr. Flack. He had been in the library on Tuesday night, reading microfilm. On his way out, he stopped at the circulation desk to regale her with tales of Gnosticism throughout the ages. According to him, Gnostics believed in a goddess, Sophia, and a variety of gods.

Beth was beginning to wonder how she could stem his verbosity so she could get back to studying for tomorrow's classes when his soliloquy on the nearly two centuries of Gnosticism—from its beginnings to the fairly recent finding of scrolls found in Nag Hammadi, in Egypt, which were not yet fully translated—was interrupted by a phone call from a patron pleading for an extension on her due date.

Beth strung out the phone call, taking her time digging the cards out of the due date file and penciling in the new dates, hoping Mr. Flack would take the hint. Unfortunately, he did not. As soon as she hung up, he resumed his lecture. When he mentioned some citations he needed to check, Beth seized the chance to redirect the conversation.

She told him that she would be happy to pick up some books for him, if he called the NDSC librarian in advance and made the arrangements. She'd no sooner spoken than he jumped at her offer. So, here she was, lugging an armload of books across campus. He said he would return to the library tonight to pick them up. She left his books, as well as her backpack, in the car when she stopped at home to feed Chestnut and change clothes for work.

Chestnut greeted her happily when she came into the kitchen through the back door. He crunched through his supper and then leaped up on her lap for an afternoon nap, while she fortified herself with a few cookies and a cup of instant coffee. She needed something stronger than tea today.

As she petted Chestnut, she told him, "It's already been a long week, and it's not over, yet."

When the phone rang, Chestnut jumped off her lap and ran out of the room. Beth let it ring and considered not answering it. But, decided she better. What if it were important?

"Hello."

"Hi, you are home." It was Bill Crample.

"Yup, I'm here. What's up?" Beth said. This was the second time he'd called within a week. She hoped he wasn't going to make a habit of it.

"Just thought I'd give you an update. We picked up Allen Peterson."

"You did? When was this?"

"This afternoon. He was crossing over from Grand Bend to the Minnesota side. We figured if he was still in the area, it wouldn't be long until we spotted him. There are only so many ways to cross the river, and that purple car is a real eye-catcher. So, you don't have to worry about him popping up."

"Okay, thanks. You know..."

"What?" he prompted her.

"I was just wondering if you would be interested in coming to a Library Supporter's meeting?"

There was a pause. "Why would I want to do that? That's a bit outside of my area of interest," he said.

"Okay, well never mind," she said.

"Hang on, tell me more. What's the purpose of this meeting?" he said.

"Mostly, to get the suspects together. I just don't think that Al is the guilty party. I think he did care for Crystal, in his warped way, or at least appreciated that she was a money maker. Why would he kill her?"

"Because she was going to leave him. Of course, he says he didn't do it. That he was on his way to Fargo to meet up with some friends at the time. Of course, we'll check out his movements. But, any buddies of his are likely not the most reliable characters."

"Okay, that makes sense. I just think there are other, stronger suspects. But, I won't try to convince you. How about this. I'll ask Miss Tanner to send you an invitation to the meeting, it's going to be at her house, and you can decide if you want to come or not. Okay?"

He paused, then said, "Sure, I guess that'd be okay. Thanks."

"No problem," she said. "Thanks for letting me know about Al's arrest."

Beth sat at the circulation desk, stamping due date cards for tomorrow. Once the cards were stamped, she glanced through her backpack but didn't feel inspired to dive into anything. Nothing was due, and she always worked best under a deadline. She admitted that she was something of a procrastinator. She started leafing through the pile of books she'd schlepped over for Mr. Flack. *He'd better show up*, she thought, *after she'd made the effort to get them here for him.* She started to thumb through one titled *Gnosticism and Early Christianity.*

She was reading a section on Simon Magnus when Mr. Flack arrived. In spite of the new entryway, he arrived in a wave of cold air.

"Hello there, Mr. Flack," Beth said, glad to see him. It was beginning to be a little too quiet in the library. It was a bitterly cold night, so that must have kept people home. Only a few patrons had stopped by. "I have your books from the NDSC library right here. I was glancing through them, and happened to run across this section on Simon Magnus."

"Oh, yes, believed by many to be the father of Gnosticism. He was mentioned in the Bible, you know, in the Acts of the Apostles, I believe."

"Is that right? So it goes back that far," Beth said.

She realized that her question probably revealed that she hadn't been listening to him when he was last in on Tuesday night. But, she hoped he wouldn't mind repeating himself. Apparently, he didn't mind, and he launched into another description of the history of Gnosticism.

When he stopped for air, she asked, "You mentioned that there is a local group of Gnostics. What's that all about?"

"A good question," he said. "I am attempting to find out more, myself. I want to include some first-hand observations in the book I'm working on, but I've been stymied. I was invited to a special Gnostic mass, but, at the last minute it was called off."

"When was that supposed to occur?" Beth asked.

"On the night of the winter solstice," he said. "It is a special night to some Gnostics. All about the return of the light, and so on."

Beth felt a tingle go up her spine. "It was called off? Do you know why?"

"My source said that the virgin, who is integral to the celebration, was suddenly not available. Of course, it's not always an actual virgin, just a young girl. Virgins are not that easy to find these days, I suppose." He laughed.

"Who is your source?" she asked.

"I'm sorry. I can't say. Sworn to secrecy, and all that. If there's anything a secret society hates, it is having their secrets spread around." He laughed again.

She tried, without success, to get him to spill the beans. He seemed to consider it all a big joke.

"I have to protect my sources if I want to get invited to another of their little shindigs," he said.

He left with his books after thanking her, profusely for her efforts. As soon as he left, Beth grabbed up the phone, called Evie, and filled her in on what he'd said, and Al's arrest.

"I think I know why Crystal was killed," she said. "Now, we just need to figure out who did it."

Chapter 29

The folding chairs were arranged into a tight semicircle in Miss Tanner's living room. Everyone invited had accepted the invitation, intrigued by her description of it as a special celebration of the life and legacy of Edgar Allen Poe. Miss Tanner had dragooned her high-school helpers into acting as waitstaff and doormen, taking people's coats and other wraps as they arrived.

The guest list included the library supporters: Doctor and Mrs. Frost, Father McClure, Mr. and Mrs. Flack, Mr. Brown, Mr. and Mrs. Nobis, and Mr. and Mrs. Gloor. Beth and Evie were also guests. Rounding out the group, Captain Swensen was there.

Officer Crample stood, stiff and impassive, near the living room door. When Evie and Beth arrived he barely said hello. He didn't look happy to be there. He had called Beth last week and admitted that Allen's alibi had checked out. He had been in Fargo when Crystal was killed. Along with witness statements, he had a receipt from a gas station that proved it. However, since they had found weed in his car when they stopped him as he crossed state lines from Grand Bend, North Dakota, into Minnesota, he wasn't likely to go free any time soon.

An excited murmur of expectation rose from the guests as they milled around the edges of the semicircle, filled coffee cups from the urn on the sideboard, and helped themselves to tidbits of cheese, crackers, grapes, and tiny finger sandwiches, while they questioned each other about what they thought would happen next.

Miss Tanner, wearing her leopard skin outfit, announced, "Ladies and gentlemen, if you would take a seat, we can get underway."

Beth stood to the side, watching as everyone else took their place. Her heart was beating fast. She took a deep breath to try to calm herself. She had carefully selected an outfit that she hoped made her look both approachable but also business-like. She wore a dark-beige twill tunic vest with matching flare-leg pants, her wide-lapel white shirt, and a pair of stacked heels to give her a couple of added inches of height. She noticed that Captain Swensen took a seat on the edge of the group, where he had a good view of everyone else.

Miss Tanner went to the front of the room, faced the group, and said, "My assistant, Miss Williams, would like to present some information and ask you some questions. As you may have heard, she was the one who first discovered the body of the missing girl, Crystal Jones."

An audible gasp arose from the group.

Miss Tanner continued, "Miss Williams has been assisting the police in their efforts to find out who is responsible for Crystal's death. Please help her as much as you can."

With that, she sat down and Beth took Miss Tanner's place. She had been nervous about speaking in front of them. Public speaking was something she dreaded, but she was surprised to notice that she felt pretty calm. She smiled at Evie, who smiled back at her. That made her feel better.

"Thank you for coming," she said. "First of all, I want to tell you what happened, and what I know. There are still missing pieces. Hopefully, you can help fill some of those in for me."

She related when, and how, she found the body, how the body had gone missing, and how they had found the ring near the scene of the crime.

"Eventually, my brother found her body outside of town, as many of you may know. Someone had dumped her by the side of the road, where the highway turns toward Grand Bend. I guess many of you have probably dumped stuff off there, too. But I don't expect you to admit it now."

A nervous titter ran through the group.

"Since Crystal was killed near the railroad station, it was logical to assume she was either arriving or leaving. I checked with the station master. He remembered her buying a ticket to the cities. Evie and I started to piece together what had led up to her death. Crystal's living arrangement wasn't good. The man she was living with, Allen Peterson, had been trafficking her, sexually."

This was greeted with stunned silence.

"Our investigation indicated that Allen had made some sort of arrangement with the manager of the Big Boy Restaurant. He was dropping his girls there, and then their customers were picking them up. I won't go into the details of the arrangement at this time."

"Girls, plural?" asked Captain Swensen.

"Yes," Beth said. "Two other girls joined the household this past fall. That is what, I believe, precipitated Crystal's desire to leave Allen for good. She'd attempted to leave him on other occasions, but had ended up going back to him. That's what made him our chief suspect for a while. But he has an alibi that clears him.

"I found some evidence that Miss Jones had been planning her exit for some time. It included a bank book with a series of deposits and one large withdrawal near the time she planned to leave. I wondered what she was doing at the bank. I understand she was talking to you, Mr. Brown. Perhaps you could enlighten us."

"Yes, of course. It's nothing out of the ordinary. I spoke to her when she opened an account with us. Later, she looked into obtaining a safe deposit box, but then decided against it."

"I see. At the same time that I found her bank book, I also found a postcard from a woman who had expected her to arrive in the cities on the night of December 21st. The night she died. Later, I learned that she was Crystal's half-sister. They had the same father. And, he had sent Crystal a fairly large sum of money. Previously, he had refused to acknowledge her as his daughter, but he had decided to make amends. Having another source of income probably also figured into Crystal's decision to leave Allen, and make a new life for herself.

"Another item in her possession was a letter from her attorney, Mr. Nobis. Perhaps you can share with us how you came to represent her, and what was in that letter.

Mr. Nobis scrutinized Beth, eyes narrowed. Beth guessed he was wondering why she knew about the letter, but not its contents.

"As you know, Allen is a client," he said. "I've kept him out of jail on more than one occasion. Naturally, when Miss Jones sought legal help, she approached me. I wouldn't betray a client's confidence but, since she's deceased, I see no harm in telling you that she was looking into her legal rights in regard to this man she now knew was her father. By the way, the contents of her post office box, a lead that you'd asked me to look into, were not very illuminating. They simply confirmed that Crystal was planning to leave permanently. There was another letter, or two, from her half-sister and one from her foster mother. Both offered her a place to stay while she got settled."

"I see. Thank you for looking into that," Beth said. "So we knew she was leaving, and why, and the time she left. I wanted to know more about that day. Evie and I made several trips to the Big Boy, and finally found someone who admitted to seeing her there on the afternoon of December 21st. He saw her use the payphone. So, we knew she was there, but not who picked her up. She hadn't taken a taxi; we checked. So, she must have gotten a ride."

"I wondered about Father McClure's movements. He was late to mass that evening. Later, I learned that he had picked Crystal up from the Big Boy, and his car had been seen at the railway station shortly before the time of her death."

The crowd gasped. Everyone turned and stared at the priest.

"She was alive when I left her at the station," Father McClure said.

"I'm sure that's true," Beth said.

"What I'd like to know is, who told you that I was late for mass?" Father McClure asked.

"It was Mr. Gloor," she said.

"I see," Father McClure frowned at Mr. Gloor.

Mrs. Gloor fixed her husband with a suspicious glare.

"And then," Beth continued. "There was the ring Evie and I found. It was a very odd ring, and it got us wondering what kind of ring it was. Miss Tanner's cousin, an antiquities expert for the University of Minnesota, helped us with that."

Beth looked at Miss Tanner, who nodded encouragingly.

"It turns out the stone is something called an abraxas stone, from ancient Egypt."

A murmur of excitement swept the room.

"However, the stone is common. There are many of them in circulation. But he said the metal itself was more recent, and yet, valuable. So, we turned it over to the police. As far as I know, it hasn't been claimed. Is that right, Officer Crample?" Beth said.

"No, it hasn't been claimed, yet. As far as I know."

"So, that made me wonder, why wouldn't someone report that a valuable ring was missing? Either they didn't realize it was missing or they don't want it associated with the crime."

Beth noticed Mr. Nobis looking at his right hand, seeming in deep thought.

"One puzzle piece fell into place through a conversation with our town's newspaper editor, who is writing a book on Gnostic practices.

"Mr. Flack told me that there is a local Gnostic sect, a secret society, and they were planning a winter solstice Gnostic mass, but it was called off at the last minute because the girl who was supposed to play the part of the virgin had gone missing. Am I getting that right, Mr. Flack?"

"Yes, that's correct," he said.

"That's when I knew the reason why Crystal was killed. She was supposed to be the virgin in this sacrilegious farce, and she had decided not to go through with it."

This pronouncement caused an uproar. People started to raise their voices as they talked over one another. Several people got up and started toward the door.

Captain Swensen got up and, in a commanding tone, said, "Sit down, everyone, and be quiet. Let's hear what else Miss Williams has to say."

They all resumed their seats, eyes riveted on her.

"There isn't a lot left to say," Beth said. "I know when and where Crystal was killed, and I believe I know why. But, I still don't know who did it."

Mrs. Gloor looked at her husband and said, "Larry, why did you tell her that Father McClure was late for Saturday evening mass that night. You weren't even there."

Everyone turned and looked at Mr. Gloor. He squirmed in his chair.

"You must be mistaken, dear," Mr. Gloor said. "I was there."

"You most certainly were not. We were planning to keep the store open late that evening for Christmas shoppers. I had an afternoon appointment at my hairdresser's, so you offered to stay at the store."

"Oh, yes, that's right. I was at the store. I must have been thinking of another time when Father McClure was late."

"No, that can't be right," Mr. Nobis said. "I thought you might close early, so I stopped by the store to see if my ring was ready, but the store was closed. I thought you might be in the back so I knocked repeatedly, but no one answered."

Mr. Nobis turned to Beth. "You said that you found a man's ring, white gold, with an abraxas stone? That's my ring, but I didn't lose it. Mr. Gloor had it. He was repairing the attachment prongs, which were coming loose. Later, he said he had to send it out for special work and hadn't gotten it back yet." He turned to Mr. Gloor and said, "You still haven't returned that ring."

Everyone turned and looked at Mr. Gloor again.

Beth walked over, stood in front of Mr. Gloor, and pulled the St. Christopher's medal she'd bought at the church out of her pocket and dangled it in front of him. "You sell these at your store. One of these was found around Crystal's neck when her body was found. Did you give it to her?"

Mr. Gloor blanched. He jumped up, knocking over his chair with a bang, and bolted toward the door.

Bill Crample stepped in front of him. "Where do you think you're going?" he asked.

Mr. Gloor's shoulders slumped. He turned back toward the crowd, his face fell, and he looked like he might cry. "She wouldn't come back."

Mr. Gloor turned to Father McClure. "I saw you, with her. I was heading out to the Big Boy to pick her up. I saw you going the other way and I followed you. I knew I couldn't show up without Crystal. Everyone was counting on me. I waited until you left and then I tried to talk to her."

He turned to Mr. Nobis. "I offered her your ring if she would just stay for one more day. I had it in my pocket. I was going to give it to you before the meeting. Sorry, Fredrick, it was the only valuable thing I had to give her. I tried to explain the importance of the ceremony. That it was the one time, on the night of the winter solstice, when the sex magic was most powerful. She wouldn't listen. She just took the ring from me and threw it into the snow. She shouted at me—called me names. Can you imagine? Her—a girl like that—shouting at me? I lost my head, just for a moment."

He held his hands up in front of his face. "I grabbed her neck and squeezed and squeezed. I didn't mean to do it. When I let go, she wasn't breathing. I didn't know what to do. I threw her body down the hill, hoping it might look like an accident. Then, I saw someone, down there, looking up at me. That must have been you, Beth."

She nodded mutely, spellbound by the vision of the timid jeweler transformed into a crazed killer.

"I had to think of someplace else to take her. I drove to the bottom of the hill, put her body in the trunk, and drove around, frantically. Finally, I dumped her body down the culvert by the river. On top of the trash. God! It was awful. I couldn't sleep after that. Oh, my God. What have I done?"

He picked up his chair and collapsed into it. "I'm glad it's over. At least now, maybe I can get some sleep." He put his head into his hands and sobbed.

Captain Swensen and Officer Crample, one on each side, helped him up and led him out of the room.

It was Saturday afternoon, the day after Valentine's Day. Beth sat in her mother's kitchen and watched as she prepared the meringue for her lemon meringue pie.

"Mom, you are a true artist," Beth said. "Nobody makes pies like you do."

"Flattery will get you nothing, except a piece of pie," her mom said. "But, not until Gary and Debbie get here."

"What's the occasion?" Beth asked.

"I don't know. They're being very mysterious. I guess we'll find out soon enough."

"Who's being mysterious," Cathy said as she popped her head into the kitchen.

"Gary and Debbie are being mysterious. They announced they are coming over, and Mom is making a pie to mark the occasion."

"Oh, yum," Cathy said. She jangled her charm bracelet in front of Beth. "I'm still wearing it. See?"

"Yes, I'm glad you like it and haven't lost it, yet," Beth said.

"I never lose stuff, and it's a good thing because, now that Gloor's Jewelry Store is closed, I don't know when I'll get another charm for my bracelet. What about you? Did you ever find that ring you were looking for?"

"Yup, I found it," Beth said, recalling it with an inward shudder.

"That was so weird, how old Mr. Gloor killed that girl, and that crazy cult and everything. I read all about it in the newspaper when he was arrested. Why do you suppose he did it?" Cathy said.

"I don't know. I think it must have been a sort of temporary insanity," Beth said. "But, it's all behind us now. And that sect is gone, too. Nothing spoils a secret cult like making it public."

Beth had told her sister as little as possible about the whole case, to spare her the details. Besides, she wanted to put it behind her, too. She had enough to worry about between her classes, her apartment, her job, taking care of Chestnut, and now Bill Crample. He had called her, asking her to go out with him. Maybe she should just say yes, once. They'd go out, and then realize they had nothing in common, and that would be the end of it. But, she didn't want to complicate her life.

Beth heard a car pull up and park in the driveway. Her dad went out and preceded Gary and Debbie back into the house.

"Hi, everyone," Gary said. "And, how's our little Miss Marple?" he said to Beth. "Have you heard the latest about the fire at Al's house?"

"No, what about it?" Beth asked.

"They say it was caused by a faulty space heater. Apparently, it fell over, failed to turn off, and set something on fire," Gary said.

"So, when Sam fought with Al it might have gotten knocked over," Beth said.

"What's this all about? Sam fought with Al?" Cathy said, her eyes bright with curiosity.

"Yeah," Gary started, and then noticed Beth glaring at him and changed the subject. "Speaking of Sam, did you hear that Sam is dating Bev?"

"Bev? Bev who?" Mom said, suspending a slice of pie midway between the pie plate and the individual plates. "Come on, sit down everyone and have some pie."

"You know," Gary said. "Bev, from the bank."

"Oh my, I never would have put those two together. Well, I wish them the best of luck," Mom said as she distributed slices of pie. "And now, you've kept us in the dark long enough," she scolded Gary. "What's the big news?"

Gary motioned for Debbie to take center stage. "I have some good news and some bad news for you, Mr. and Mrs. Williams," she said.

"Call me Mom. I keep telling you that. Bad news? Oh no, what is it?"

"The bad news is that soon you'll have to start making bigger pies, or more of them," Debbie said, beaming.

"What? Why?"

"That's the good news," Gary said. "Stop beating around the bush, Debbie. Mom, you're going to be a Grandma. Debbie and I are going to have a baby."

Biography

Bonnie Oldre has always loved books. One of her prized childhood possessions was her library card. She remembers summer afternoons at the library, turning pages with fingers wrinkled after hours spent playing in the adjacent city swimming pool. While reading, she was transported to a whole new world of adventure and information. She was interested in everything.

Bonnie is a retired librarian who lives in Minneapolis, Minnesota, with her husband, Randy Oldre, and pet tabby cat, Chocolate. She has a B.A. in English Literature and an M.L.I.S. degree. When not writing, she enjoys a variety of activities, including reading, singing in a chorale, gardening, and more. *Silent Winter Solstice* is her debut novel.

63222782R00173